To Baylie & Marvin,
Want to grow up and be like you—
You are my inspiration!
Hugs,
Mara

the Stockbroker

Insider Information

J.R. Shine

ISBN: 1468146955
ISBN 13: 9781468146950
Library of Congress Control Number: 2012900040
CreateSpace Independent Publishing Platform
North Charleston, South Carolina

I dedicate this book to my husband, Gerard. Thank you for your loving patience, support and eternal positive attitude. You make my dreams come true.

4 Stars (out of 5)

What if *Sex and the City*'s Carrie Bradshaw came from a wealthy family and became a stockbroker? That might be overstating it a bit, but chick lit does meet finance in J.R. Shine's difficult-to-put-down novel *The Stockbroker: Insider Information.*

Jennifer Palmer, the stockbroker of the book's title, is a recent college graduate, young and inexperienced. After breaking off her engagement to a suitor she doesn't really love, Jennifer moves home to finish college and begins a career in the rough-and-tumble world of finance. Against all odds, Jennifer finds good fortune in love and money—but it may all be a bit too good to be true.

Having worked at major investment firms for nearly thirty years, Shine knows her topic well. Anyone familiar with the stockbroker trade will recognize plenty of note-perfect details.

Similarly, Shine fills her writing with fun asides about other topics she knows well: food, fashion, and the South Florida lifestyle.

Glitz and glamour are present throughout the book—meals are gourmet, and fashion accoutrements are expensive.

Fortunately, Shine deftly balances the fine line between allowing readers to live vicariously through Jennifer, with her Hermes Birkin handbag and Manolo Blahnik shoes, while at the same time not dismissing her as a spoiled brat. It is fun to catch the designer name-dropped throughout the book, but it is easier to cheer for Jennifer when she is braving a crass, male-dominated field and battling everything from her parents' expectations to the "no mercy" approach to investing at her firm to the wealthy Russian oligarch determined that Jennifer be his girlfriend.

The novel features a breezy style that keeps the reader feeling as swept up in Jennifer's adventures as she is. With Jennifer flying in a private Gulfstream jet, Shine writes: "The sound of the engine lulled her into a light sleep only to be awakened by the smell of food cooking in the galley. The stewardess came by with the shrimp cocktail." A few minutes later, Jennifer is enjoying lobster and expensive wine on her way to the story's exciting conclusion.

The Stockbroker: Insider Information is an enjoyable book. The once-naive Jennifer Palmer gets a thorough education, ending this adventure a wiser, more mature young woman.

If Shine has another *Stockbroker* tale in her, readers will certainly be eager to join Jennifer for the next chapter of her life.

ForeWord Clarion Review

Chapter 1

It was a crystal clear evening in St. Tropez, the stars were glistening, and a magnificent moon lit up the smooth as velvet Mediterranean Sea. A slight breeze carried the rich scent of lavender wafting across the Provencal countryside creating a special romantic atmosphere.

The temperature was perfect for a moonlit party on the deck of one of the largest private yachts ever built, "The Stoli," owned by the biggest vodka producer in the world. Jennifer was in her cabin getting dressed for the night's activities. The cabin was oversized and ornately decorated, with mirrors on the walls as well as on the ceilings. In fact, in the back of her mind, Jennifer had a vague suspicion that the mirrors might be two-way, and she was being watched. There was a Jacuzzi tub at the foot of her bed. The bathroom was likewise large and ostentatious, appointed with Bulgari toiletries including soaps, shampoo, conditioner, a luxurious skin cream and the wonderful Parfum de Bulgari. It was all green marble, with two large sinks adorned with solid gold faucets. The shower could easily fit a party of three with water spouts coming out of walls, spraying every part of her beautiful body. As lavish as her accommodations were, Jennifer felt uneasy and a bit on edge.

Earlier in the day she'd been taken ashore by a launch to see the city, to practice her French and do a little shopping. She'd protested when she was told that two bodyguards would be accompanying her, but was told that it was for her own protection. So off she had gone with two goons in tow, stopping in at Longchamp to pick up a handbag, then on to Cavalli's to try on some of their signature animal print jeans. Jennifer found just the right pair that accentuated her long, lean body. Since she hardly ever ate during the day, before going into La Ligne to purchase some typical Provencal linen, she visited the bakery next door, buying a warm and crusty baguette. All this time, the goons had not left her side. At one point, while on the launch, she had taken out her I-phone to call her parents and her secretary back at the office in Florida. When her two brutish companions saw her taking out her cell, they immediately took it from her, saying, "No phone calls, we'll return this to you later." With that, Jennifer was alerted. Something didn't seem right to her, but maybe this was the way the ultra-rich protected their friends. Still, something was very strange and Jennifer's intuition told her that she needed to unravel this situation she had gotten herself into, sooner than later.

Back in her cabin still sans cell phone, Jennifer had just slipped into her beautiful evening gown. It was a yellow jersey Lauren Black Label, which clung to her exquisite, shapely form. She knew that there would be beautiful women attending the party, but Jennifer was no shrinking violet. She stood 5'10", with long blonde flowing-straight hair, crystal blue eyes and flawless fair skin. Jennifer created a presence wherever she went, but the nice thing was that she didn't know it. She had gorgeous long legs, an ample bust and a tiny waist. Her dresses were size 0, but they were always still big. Everything she bought was taken right to her seamstress to ensure a perfect fit. She always accentuated her positives, opting for a dress or skirt, adorned with her signature look, a Hermes scarf draped casually around her shoulders.

Jennifer was athletic in a feminine kind of way. She loved to play tennis, bicycle and horseback ride, preferably dressage. Jennifer always behaved like a lady, reflecting her background and what she had accomplished in life. She was financially independent, owning a wraparound condo beachside in Palm Beach, along with a chalet in Aspen, where she loved to escape the Florida heat in the summer. She had a penchant for cars, currently owning a white Austin Martin and a BMW 6 Crossover X for her "girls." These were the two loves of her life, "Jackie O," a white Standard Poodle and "Lola," a cozy little Bichon Frise. Jennifer was a true success story – beauty, brains and all of the toys that went along with the good life.

Jennifer could hear the party already getting started on the upper decks. A series of helicopters were landing on the top deck pad, delivering happy partygoers. The band was playing the music of her beloved disco era and she could hear glasses faintly clinking as toasts were already being made.

From the veranda of her cabin, Jennifer had seen the young girls stepping up to the yacht as the various launches dropped them off. They were wearing thigh-high designer dresses with their breasts reaching for the sky and requisite red soled Louboutin shoes. The men were wearing tuxedos, some with white jackets and some with the de rigueur black jacket and a pair of bun revealing blue jeans very tight in the crotch area. No socks of course, just the standard Gucci or Tod loafers.

She completed her ensemble with a pair of gold, strappy Blahniks. Despite the fact that Jennifer was in her twenties, she knew that she outshone all of the "eurotrash" wannabes.

After grabbing her gold-threaded pashmina and Leiber clutch she opened her cabin door only to be greeted by her newfound goons. Apparently, unbeknownst to her, they were standing guard outside her cabin. As they escorted her to the party, Jennifer knew that she had to come up with an exit strategy very soon. First her cell phone was taken from her and now she was being treated as though she were a bird in a gilded cage.

Jennifer and her entourage made their way up to the pool deck, where the party was in full swing. On the way, from the corner of her eye, Jennifer noticed a small black dinghy motoring toward the yacht. When they arrived on the "party deck," there was an array of attractive guests as well as a lavish display of food. Everything and anything you could imagine, the centerpiece was a blue tin of Ossetra caviar. Surrounding the caviar were the delectable riches from the sea: clams, mussels, bright red lobsters, grilled prawns, bouillabaisse...with all the accoutrements. On the other side of the deck, a dessert table had been set up with the most delicious French patisseries: tarte tartin, macaroons, madeleines, éclairs, tartelettes de framboises, crème brulee and more. Immediately next to the dessert table, the yacht's chefs were prepping sauté pans for cherries jubilee and crepes Suzette. The two bars were already loaded with thirsty guests. Every kind of beverage was available. To start the evening, the guests were served Cristal poured into Baccarat flutes. The highlight of the bar was a vodka fountain out of which flowed the yacht owners' drink of choice: his personal elixir fermented from the best wheat mash Soviet Georgia had to offer. Jennifer took in the scene. It was straight out of a Hollywood movie. And she definitely was one of the stars. As she sauntered over to the bar to get herself a glass of champagne, her host, Dimitri, approached her with a big smile. Not only was his smile big, but his corpus was as well. He was wearing a light blue silk shirt unbuttoned practically down to his navel. Thick strands of gold necklaces were draped over his hairy chest. One held a large medallion covered in diamonds. He wore white linen pants and blue velvet slippers adorned with his initials in a crest over the tip. "How is my American guest enjoying herself? I told you that once you got to know me better, you would appreciate me!"

Jennifer was relieved to finally see him. She told him that everything was lovely, but why did she have bodyguards?

He replied, "My darrrling, not to worry. This is how I take care of my friends." With that, he gave her a light kiss on her lips and ambled off to greet the other guests. Jennifer took her glass of champagne and walked over to the railing to look out at the lights of St. Tropez twinkling in the distance.

Suddenly, a movement caught her eye, the black dinghy that she had seen before was approaching midship. She could see three men in black wetsuits, their faces covered, throwing ropes up to the boat. This gave them the ability to secure the dinghy and climb aboard the ship. Maybe these were pirates, Jennifer thought coming on board to rob the guests...or maybe they were looking to take possession of the yacht, guests and all, and demand a ransom. Jennifer was highly concerned to say the least. Despite her agitation, she suddenly realized that this might be the exit strategy she had hoped for. She looked to see where her goons were, and spotted them on the other side of the deck, looking quite inebriated and running their paws over a couple of sexy girls wearing skin tight spandex dresses. Good, she thought, maybe just maybe she could subtly escape.

Before she knew it, all hell was breaking loose, the men in wetsuits were on the deck with guns hanging across their chests, shouting commands to the guests in French to get on the floor. Bedlam ensued. Jennifer had been standing apart from the crowd behind the bridge. This was her chance to get away. Though she had no money and all her belongings were in her cabin, Jennifer knew that she had to make a move, now or never. Eluding the pirates she fled to the lowest deck where she saw their dinghy tied up. Happily, the watercraft was floating in the water at the same level as the yacht. She gingerly lifted up her yellow gown and quietly lowered herself into the small vessel. Jennifer had never been in a dinghy before, but recalled how the yacht's mates had started the launch earlier in the day. She appraised the controls and saw oars, quickly determining that it would be better to row away from the yacht, before turning on the engine. Hopefully, by rowing away, she would not draw any attention her way.

When she was about thirty feet away from the yacht, she flipped on the motor, racing over the ink-blue sea to freedom. Was she about to get into deeper trouble than she already was in? Maybe her nightmare was coming to an end, or maybe this would be the second chapter. No matter what, Jennifer knew that she had to get off that yacht. If not, her instincts told her that something bad was about to happen... and Jennifer's instincts were never wrong.

Chapter 2

Even though she was born in the "cocaine cowboy" days of South Florida, Jennifer was brought up the old-fashioned European way. She was taught to always present herself as a lady, respecting her elders and never using profanity. As a child, her mother and French governess taught her French, before fully learning English.

Every summer, when school was out, she was taken to Europe for a family vacation. They would reside in different locales on the continent, so she would be exposed to different cultures. What really intrigued Jennifer about travel was tempting her palate with different food samples. As she got older, she would look forward to returning home and trying out new dishes on her friends. Each summer while in Europe, her parents also bought her a new wardrobe for the upcoming year. Jennifer adored the shopping selection in Europe. The outfits sold in the stores there were so different from the merchandise available in the United States.

Jennifer attended prep school back home and was required to wear a uniform, but was able to break-out her new European wardrobe on weekends and holidays. Her classmates found her to be a bit aloof and standoffish. They simply didn't understand that Jennifer was just painfully shy. She never quite seemed to fit in at school, opting to skip lunch with the others and study in the library.

Her parents, both physicians, always encouraged Jennifer to maintain her independence, especially financially. When Jennifer turned 13, her parents gifted her $50,000 to invest in the stock market, of course, under their supervision. In fact, her father would take her to their stockbroker's office so she could discuss her investment selections with him. Jennifer loved these visits. She was so impressed with the broker and all the trappings that came with the job. He was someone who had really earned her respect.

In school, Jennifer was expected to have straight A's and attend a prestigious college, just like her parents. Her mother attended the University of Lausanne in Switzerland and her dad was a Harvard graduate. Sometimes her parents drove her crazy with their expectations. They even demanded that she socialize with certain friends, and of course, they never approved of any young man that she brought home. They had a talent for making the young man feel totally uncomfortable, embarrassing their daughter.

To escape her parents, Jennifer turned to modeling during her free time in high school and college. Usually for the regional department stores, strutting down the runway or appearing in print ads. This was a world that she knew her parents couldn't even begin to relate to. During her high school and college years, she loved to go discoing. Typically her dates were the gays she would meet through modeling. They were always fun, great dancers and definitely safe.

Graduating with a 4.0 grade average from prep school, Jennifer went on to college at Emory in Atlanta, Georgia. She had planned to go into pre-med and become a physician, just like her parents. Unfortunately, college calculus blocked her way. Her parents hired countless tutors to teach her the course, but Jennifer could not comprehend the abstract numbers and symbols. Without a passing grade in calculus, pre-med was out of the question. Jennifer had to choose a new educational path. She would have loved a Communications major, and work in TV, but her practical side told her that the competition was fierce in that arena. So, since she had learned about investing and was always so impressed with the family's stockbroker, she selected Economics as her new path to a successful career. Jennifer enjoyed her classes and kept the vision of working at an elite brokerage firm foremost in her mind.

Jennifer would frequently fly down south, coming home on weekends and holidays. Over Christmas break, she came home for a month. Upon her arrival, her parents were especially upbeat. As it turned out, they had befriended a new resident at the hospital. They had gotten to know him quite well and felt that he would be a perfect match for their beloved daughter. Despite Jennifer's protestations, they had arranged for him to call Jennifer and invite her out to dinner. She reluctantly agreed to meet him, only because she really wasn't dating anyone on a regular basis. She was just too involved with her studies to be distracted. The young resident's name was Brook Franklin. When he phoned her they had a lively conversation. She was curious as to his specialty, and was delighted to find out that it was Plastic Surgery. Well, she thought that this would be an interesting date. At worst, she could pick his brain as to the latest techniques in ageless beauty. Brook came to the house at 7:00 to take Jennifer out to dinner. She wore her standard LBD with white pearls and noted that Brook was all dressed up. He had on a cashmere navy blazer, blue and white striped, open shirt with cufflinks and beige trousers. Jennifer had been around doctors all her life, and knew that they didn't have a clue as to how to dress. He was even wearing Guccis and was fairly handsome in a swarthy kind of way. Brook had an olive complexion, good skin, his own hair and was tall enough so she wouldn't loom over him with her strappy stilettos. Jennifer was actually pleasantly surprised that he had been her parents' pick.

They walked out of the house together to his car, a white Mercedes SL500, so far so good, Jennifer thought. Brook drove to Café Charisse, one of Jennifer's favorite French restaurants. Her parents must have told him how much she enjoyed French cuisine. He has reserved a table in the corner, away from the maddening crowd. He really wanted to get to know this beautiful young lady. Brook insisted on ordering. In a way, Jennifer liked the fact that he took the initiative but at the same time, she thought it was slightly pretentious. He didn't even ask her what she might like. Nevertheless, he ordered a decent menu: escargots to start, a simple green salad, lamb chops (at least the waiter asked her how she would like them prepared), and for dessert, a chocolate soufflé with crème Anglaise. Despite the fact that Brook took control, Jennifer had a fairly nice evening. They lingered at the restaurant until its closing. While they waited for the valet, Brook slipped his hand into Jennifer's. His touch reminded her of her father's hands with their doctor's touch. Jennifer was thinking that even though this was her parents doing maybe it wasn't so bad.

Chapter 3

Jennifer and Brook dated off and on over the next several months. Either she would fly home or he would fly up to Atlanta.

It had been six months since their first date and they were dining at China Grill on South Beach, one of Jennifer's favorite spots. She loved going to restaurants where she could have food that was difficult to prepare at home. Unfortunately, as the months had gone by, Brook was getting to be so predictably boring. He really was a nice guy, but just not for her. Jennifer felt zero chemistry towards him. He was good looking, had all the right components, but Jennifer just wasn't physically attracted to him. She could barely even kiss him. Despite his predictability, when the dessert course arrived, Floating Island Asian style, Jennifer took a bite of the meringue and something un-meringue like was in her mouth. She pulled the spoon out of mouth, and noticed a sparkle. All the while, Brook was just staring at her with a silly grin on his face. It was the moment she had thought about, with dread, the sparkle turned out to be an engagement ring. One with an oversized solitaire diamond. Jennifer thought that it must have been at least 3 carats. Brook kept staring at her. "Well?" he said.

"Well what," she said, knowing what he was about to say.

"Jennifer, will you marry me?" Even though Jennifer had seen this coming, she was so taken aback that all she could do was nod, yes. Brook came over to her side of the table, and gave her a long wet kiss. "I promise you, Jennifer, I will make you happy for the rest of your life."

Jennifer was thinking, what on earth have I gotten myself into? With that, Brook stood up, took Jennifer's hand and said, "Let's go home and tell your parents the good news." Needless to say, her parents were ecstatic with the announcement. They couldn't have been happier.

Chapter 4

The next day, Jennifer was due back at school. Her parents drove her to the airport, discussing plans for the pending wedding. They thought it best to have a June wedding, right after Jen finished her sophomore year at Emory. They asked her when she intended to come down next so that they would have her input for the wedding. She told them that she trusted their judgment. And to go ahead and select the venue as well as make all the detailed decisions. Her only request was that the colors of the event be pink and green (very Lilly).

As the car approached the airline drop-off zone, Jennifer gathered her belongings and dashed off to catch her plane back to sanity.

During the flight back to Atlanta, Jennifer assumed that since she was getting married, this would be her last year attending Emory. She would have to move back to South Florida, and probably finish college at the University of Miami. What a drag, she thought; the U of M didn't have half the clout of Emory, especially when it came time to go out searching the job market. But she also knew that her parents really wanted her to marry Brook, and they had done so much for her, the least she could do in return was to satisfy their desires for their daughter's future. But on the other hand, spending the rest of her life with Brook was probably the most depressing thing she could think of.

As time went on, the wedding date was closing in on Jennifer. The semester was over on May 25 and her wedding day was June 15th. Her parents had planned a beautiful wedding at the Breakers Hotel in Palm Beach. The ceremony was to take place right on the beach at sunset, to be followed by a candle-lit dinner in the ballroom. The centerpieces that they had selected were white orchids, Jennifer's favorite flower. Jennifer still hadn't picked out a wedding dress. She knew it had to be a Vera Wang, but her heart just wasn't into shopping for one.

Brook came up to see Jennifer twice in Atlanta. Each time she responded to him in the perfunctory way of the perfect fiancé engaging in pleasant conversation over dinners and pretending to plan their future together. Brook told her that he had secured a three-bedroom condo on the tony island of Fisher. He told her that it was the perfect location since it was just minutes away from the hospital where he would be completing his residency, and just 30 minutes away from the University of Miami, where Jennifer would be attaining her college degree. Jennifer loved going to Fisher Island for parties, but living there and facing the ferry at least twice a day would be a nightmare. It seemed as though nothing Brook would do could make Jennifer happy. No matter how hard she tried, she couldn't picture herself as Mrs. Brook Franklin. In fact, she hadn't even met his family yet. They were all supposed to get together with her family for dinner upon her return from Emory.

During the week of May 25th, Jennifer packed up her things and had the family's handyman drive everything back to South Florida. She flew down on the night of the 25th. Her father picked her up at the airport, happy as a lark. Little did he know how despondent his daughter was over her future. He mentioned to her that wedding gifts were awaiting her arrival at their home. Her father thought that might get a rise out of his daughter. Maybe she was just tired from the flight and emotionally exhausted from packing and bidding her friends farewell. Little did he know that Jennifer had made up her mind and was planning on having a frank discussion with her parents at breakfast the next day.

The family met for breakfast the following morning in the garden room of their beautiful home. It was glass enclosed with the seating upholstered in the bright colors of a garden. The housekeeper served them warm croissants with homemade mango jelly, along with egg white omelets and freshly squeezed orange juice. Jennifer's parents noticed that her mood had radically changed from the previous evening. She appeared to be much calmer with a smile on her face. Jennifer was actually feeling the relief of having made a lifetime decision.

From her vantage point at the table, Jennifer could see the collection of wedding gifts in the adjacent room. She knew that this discussion would be difficult, but it had to be done. Her parents were thrilled to have her home and were looking forward to the upcoming wedding festivities.

"Mommy and Daddy," Jennifer began, "I have been doing much soul searching over the past couple of months, and I honestly cannot go through with the marriage to Brook." Her parents tried to speak, but she interrupted them, "please let me finish. You instilled in me over the years about being my own woman. You gave me the best life has to offer. I know how fond you both are of Brook, but frankly, I am not. Nor will I ever be. We have zero physical chemistry, and I can barely stand to be in his company. You both have a wonderful marriage, which I have always admired. I don't want to go into marriage thinking about how and when I will be getting divorced. So I have come to the decision of canceling our wedding. I know you have both worked hard at making all the arrangements, as well as financially investing in this event. But I just can't go through with it and I hope you will respect my decision. There, I've said it, now it's your turn to speak."

To Jennifer's surprise, her parents didn't seem so surprised by her announcement. They admitted their disappointment, but maturely backed their daughter's decision. "Well," her Dad said, "we'll have to send back the gifts to the guests and Jen, and it's up to you to break the news to Brook. I imagine that you will return the ring. It's only the right thing to do. But that's up to you, darling."

Her mother said, "Since you have already enrolled at the University of Miami, I guess it would be best if you live here until you graduate."

Between having to tell Brook about her decision and knowing that she would be spending the next two years living at home, Jennifer developed a knot in the pit of her stomach.

Well, first things first, Jennifer got up from the table to call Brook and suggest they get together for lunch. She had read somewhere that it was always best to break up in a public place. That way there hopefully would be less drama. When she got Brook on the phone, she said, "Brook, I'd like together for lunch today at about noon. We need to talk."

He always had the tendency to be a bit blunt. "Jennifer, what a pleasant surprise, you never phone me to get together. How aggressive of you. I'd like to see more of this side of you. Let's meet at Tula's. And noon it will be."

She thought that Brook would end up eating his words rather than his lunch.

Jennifer arrived a few minutes late; purposely...she wanted to get this over with quickly. As she sat down, Brook noticed that she wasn't wearing her engagement ring. He was sometimes dense but he wasn't stupid. "Jennifer, did something happen to the ring?" he asked.

"Well," Jennifer said, "that actually was the reason I wanted to get together."

"Did you lose it?" he asked. "Don't tell me that you lost it!"

"Calm down, Brook. I wanted to meet with you face to face and let you know that I can't go through with the wedding. You're a lovely guy, but just not for me. I didn't lose the ring. Here it is." Jennifer handed him the red Cartier box containing the engagement ring.

A look of angst and relief reflected on his face. "I guess it's over then," he said.

"Yes," Jennifer agreed.

The look in Jennifer's eyes more than confirmed to him that it was over. Still, he tried one last time to save the relationship. "Jen, just give us some more time?"

Jennifer adamantly shook her head and said, "Brook, it's over." She was now more determined than ever to get him out of her life.

With that, Brook abruptly stood up and quickly strode out of the restaurant, ring in hand.

Jennifer felt a wave of relief flow over her body. She knew in her heart that she had made the right decision. And yes, she was getting more aggressive, and the best was yet to come.

Chapter 5

Jennifer's junior and senior years at the University of Miami were mentally unchallenging to say the least. But Jennifer viewed her time spent there as a means to an end. Needless to say, living at home curtailed her social activities to an extent. But the virtues of living with her parents translated to the luxury of having clean laundry and great meals. Her parents were extremely pleased to have their daughter back home again. To make Jennifer's life easier, they surprised her with a red, convertible BMW 338i. They told her that it was a welcome home gift.

Her parents often entertained at home and invited many of their colleagues and friends for dinner. Jennifer's mother would plan the menus and the housekeeper would prepare the meals. Invariably, the dinner discussion always turned to the topic of investing. Her parents and the guests would exchange ideas about what type of investments they preferred and how they were doing with those investments. Jennifer sensed that quite a few of the people put more emphasis on their investments rather than on their medical practices or their spouses. Not necessarily in that order. Jennifer, herself, had been keeping a close eye on the "nest egg" that her parents had given to her. With her diligent research and her father's tutelage, her portfolio had doubled in the last seven years. She had purchased conservative stocks that paid dividends. Each quarter she would receive a check from the companies in which she owned shares. These checks added up and provided Jennifer with some extra spending money. One of the virtues her parents taught Jennifer early on was the value of money. They certainly lived a lavish lifestyle but never beyond their means. They never reflected ostentatious materialism. Those values were handed down to Jennifer.

Finally, graduation day arrived and Jennifer was more than prepared to embark on a successful career. She wanted to prove to her parents what she could accomplish on her own. For a graduation gift, Jennifer's parents gave her a choice of a new car, a month in Europe or $50,000 to add to her stock portfolio. Jennifer selected the latter. Based on her prior investment performance, she was confident that the new infusion of cash would also appreciate over time. Plus, she already had a car that she loved and didn't want to waste any more time and go to Europe.

Jennifer was motivated and looking forward to launching her career. When she informed her parents that she was ready to go out and work as a stockbroker, they tried to mask their disappointment. They had aspirations for Jennifer of attending law or business school and becoming a professional. In their eyes, a stockbroker was a glorified salesman and would always be viewed as such. They wanted the best for their daughter and felt that she would be short-changing herself by not pursuing a more "respectable" (in their eyes) career. Nevertheless, Jennifer went against their better wishes and was determined to "pound the pavement," securing the very best position in a major firm where she would excel and at the same time help her clients achieve their financial goals. What Jennifer didn't realize was that the brokerage business was a man's world, and admission into the "old boy's club" would cost her dearly.

Chapter 6

Jennifer was able to secure interviews with three brokerage firms. She purposely saved the interview with the firm where she really wanted to work for last. By orchestrating this schedule, she would learn from her mistakes and be well prepared for the most important meeting.

The first firm she met with was a regional wire house. Jamison Dodd & Co was highly regarded in the state of Florida but had little national clout. They had a very small investment banking department and participated in few Initial Public Offerings (IPOs). Still, Jennifer felt that it was worth giving them a chance. As soon as she entered their offices, she was struck with the shabbiness of the place. There was no lobby or receptionist, just a large open floor, where salesmen, mostly in jeans and polo shirts were on the phone. She observed that many had their feet propped on their desks and appeared to be reading from scripts. She could hear four letter words peppering their conversations. The scene looked like a segment from the show "Sixty Minutes," where a "boiler room" operation was revealed. One of the men sitting closest to the front door put his hand on the phone receiver and asked her what she wanted. Jennifer told him that she had an appointment with the manager, Rory Cole. Surprisingly, he replied, "I'm Rory, let me just finish this pitch."

Since there was no seating area, Jennifer stood there and listened to his hard sell. At the end of the conversation, he said, "OK, Jack, I'll put you in for 50,000 shares. You'll thank me for this." After hanging up the phone he gestured for Jennifer to follow him to the back of the room where there were two empty chairs.

"Wow," Jennifer said, "that client bought a lot of shares."

"Honey," the manager said, "it was no big deal, they were priced at twenty cents a share. Now, young lady, tell me what you can do for Jamison Dodd."

Jennifer went into her presentation (which she had practiced endlessly). Rory appeared to be totally unimpressed.

After he impatiently heard her out, he said, "Sweetie, listen to me, I've got two big producers (brokerage house lingo for the advisor who makes the most commissions) here who need mucho help. I can offer you a position as their assistant, give you a marginal salary and I'm sure they'll give you a cut of their big bucks." With that Jennifer stood up and thanked Rory for his time, but told him that she was not interested in an assistant's position. "Honey," Rory shouted after her, "this will be the best offer you will get, but don't bother coming back."

As Jennifer walked out the door, she was thinking what a rude awakening that experience had been. She could never work in an atmosphere like that.

The second firm Jennifer scheduled to meet with appeared to be of a higher level than the "boiler room." They had an adequate lobby with a receptionist sitting behind a desk. She was so distracted with the number of calls coming in that she barely acknowledged Jennifer's entrance.

Finally, she looked up and said, "How may I help you, miss?"

Jennifer told her that she had a 2:00 p.m. appointment with the branch manager. The receptionist made a call and told Jennifer that Craig Kenyon would be out in a moment. After fifteen minutes of patiently waiting and listening to the receptionist field a multitude of calls, an attractive sandy haired man came out, extending his hand to Jennifer with a cursory greeting, "Jennifer, the market is crazy today, so I only have ten minutes to spend with you. If you prefer, we can reschedule."

Jennifer was in no mood to reschedule; she was there and wanted to determine if this firm was the place for her to start her career. Craig took her back to his office, the only private office she noticed on the floor. Once again, it appeared to be a large "bullpen," with brokers on the phone intently looking at their computer monitors, but at least some of this group was wearing button down shirts and ties. Jennifer wondered how they could conduct confidential business with their clients and not have any privacy.

"What's up?" Craig started. Jennifer was a bit taken aback. When she scheduled the appointment she had made it clear with his secretary that she was interviewing for a job as a stockbroker.

"Mr. Kenyon, I'm here today to inquire about a position as a broker with your firm. I have a resume to give you, but I would like to tell you a little about myself."

Kenyon motioned to her to give him her resume, saying, "I have no time for small talk, just give me the resume." He quickly glanced at it. "Jennifer, you just graduated from college, you have zero working experience, and at this point I can only offer you a position as a secretary. We'll see how that works out and maybe move you up the ladder from there. Hiring a rookie with no assets under her belt is not what our firm is looking for. You have to come to this firm fully equipped, ready to generate commissions from day one. It's the bottom line that counts. Nothing else matters."

Jennifer was flushed; she never expected an outcome like this. She was not looking for a secretarial position, plus she didn't even know how to type. Craig stood up. "Jennifer, that's my offer, take it or leave it, I have a volatile market to contend with."

Jennifer stood up, politely thanked him for his time and told him that she would let him know her decision in a few days. Based upon her last two interviews, she was scoring 0 out of two. She at least wanted to leave the door open. With that, she walked out, hoping that her last interview tomorrow with Tate Yardley would pan out better for her.

It was mid-June and a scorcher of a day. Jennifer was relieved to pull up to the security of her parents' home. They had gone to Europe for the summer, so she had the house to herself along with the housekeeper. She just wanted to go for a swim in the pool and take a nice hot shower, temporarily forgetting about her job hunting frustrations. Things definitely were not going as planned. The stock brokerage business was quite a bit more difficult to break into than she could have ever imagined. Well, tomorrow was a new day, and she knew that this final interview was her last chance.

Chapter 7

Jennifer woke up early the next day and decided to take a jog. She loved to run in the neighborhood early in the morning. Even though it was quite humid the air was fresh. People were out walking their dogs, there was little traffic and it was a good time for Jennifer to collect her thoughts. She had an 11:00 a.m. meeting with Tate Yardley, the largest brokerage firm in the world. She had done her homework for this meeting. They had over 20,000 brokers with 1,000 offices worldwide. They were founded 101 years ago and had been listed on the New York Stock Exchange for the past 45 years. Jennifer knew that she had to make a great impression. Ideally, she hoped that they would hire her as a "trainee." And then help her pass the Series 7 exam, which was required to conduct business.

After Jennifer finished her five mile run and returned home, she looked in her closet for the perfect "interview" dress. She settled on a navy St. John Knit. She picked out a gold butterfly pin to attach to the dress's collar and styled her long blond hair up in a ponytail. She decided on a gold Cartier watch her parents had bought for her during their last trip to France. It had always brought her good luck. And now she definitely needed all the luck she could find.

Tate Yardley was located on Brickell Avenue near downtown Miami. The branch was housed in a modern glass twenty-five story building. It occupied the penthouse floor with offices overlooking Biscayne Bay. Jennifer opened the heavy mahogany door to their offices promptly at 11:00. The reception lobby had a beautiful Oriental rug covering the light wooden floor and modern Mondrianesqe paintings hanging on the wall. As soon as she walked in she had the sense of belonging. Over the receptionist's chair were paintings of William Yardley and Cornelius Tate. The pretty brunette receptionist sitting at a Louis Quatorze desk welcomed Jennifer with a smile and asked her whom she was there to see?

Jennifer proceeded to tell her that, "I'm Jennifer Palmer and I have an 11:00 appointment with Lowell Abbott."

The receptionist said, "You're right on time, let's see if Mr. Abbott is." With that she rang him up and apparently was told that he would be out shortly. "Ms. Palmer, please take a seat, Mr. Abbott will be out in a few minutes."

Jennifer sat down on a rich brown butter leather sofa next to a thick glass table. It had several issues of the *Wall Street Journa*l on it as well *Architectural Digest, Smart Money* and *Departures* magazines. To the right of the sofa was an aquarium back lit with a soft light and brightly colored tropical fish swimming around in it. So far, this meeting seemed to be a sharp contrast from the previous two. Just when Jennifer picked up the front section of *The Wall Street Journal*, an older woman came out introducing herself as Estelle, Mr. Abbott's personal secretary. She was there to escort Jennifer back to Mr. Abbott's office. Jennifer followed Estelle down a long corridor of glass paneled offices. They were all private offices with windows overlooking the Bay. They passed a small, intimate conference room as well as a bigger conference room with about 30 chairs in it. Jennifer assumed that was the room where the branch meetings were held. Mostly men occupied the offices. They were nicely dressed and reminded Jennifer of her father's broker. The last office in the line was much bigger in scale, also with glass walls. Estelle motioned for Jennifer to go in. She was greeted by a tall, distinguished looking man with salt and pepper hair. Jennifer noticed that he was wearing a custom made sky blue shirt with initials monogrammed on his cuffs. He had on the silver Charvet tie along with the classic Gucci loafers. Upon seeing Jennifer, he immediately stood up from his desk, walked over and warmly greeted her. As she took a seat, Jennifer glanced around the large office and observed frames with photos of Lowell with past presidents, various politicians and an assortment of actors and actresses. On another wall were plaques honoring him as manager and broker of the year for the past 11 years. Jennifer was quite impressed. She felt as though she were meeting with an accomplished individual with whom she would like to work.

Instead of sitting behind his desk, Lowell took a seat on the couch adjacent to her chair. Jennifer's beauty and class were not wasted on Lowell. He knew that she not only looked money, she was money. Hiring her could be his "hole in one." He was also taken with her alluring look and in this business that could be an important asset. Lowell's eyes were locked into pursuing her shapely long legs and her stunning figure. This had not gone unnoticed on Jennifer, she felt as though he were undressing her with his eyes.

Even though Lowell was happily dating his girlfriend of nine years, he was not against getting a little action on the side. He liked his position of power over his employees. He felt his testosterone starting to boil. It made his job that much easier to have a very attractive female under his command. He really didn't give a damn about her background; he knew her ass fit the job description. But, he had to play the interview game with her.

Lowell started by saying, "Jennifer, we conducted a background check of you. This is normal procedure with all individuals who are pursuing employment with Tate Yardley. We were pleasantly surprised to see that you are related to the Palmers of Greenwich, Connecticut. I believe your uncle and I had previously met at the Robin Hood Benefit in New York City. Last year, from what I recall, your uncle was one of the group's largest benefactors. He is a true legend in the field of medicine. I read that he developed and patented the laser used in pediatric cardiac surgery. So many young lives have been saved by his research. I understand that your parents are also physicians."

Jennifer nodded, thinking that this firm really did their homework.

Lowell went on. "You come from such a rich background and we are so honored to have you consider working for our firm."

Jennifer was a bit taken aback by these accolades. This was only her third interview ever, and her potential boss was lavishing her with so many praises. Frankly, Jennifer thought it a bit odd if not premature. He hadn't even taken a look at her resume. All Lowell kept speaking about was her family background. Her Uncle Frank (her mother's brother), was indeed quite a successful physician/inventor. He had sold out his laser device to Johnson and Johnson for a large fortune. He retired from the daily practice of medicine, but lectured around the world and was known for his philanthropy, especially focusing on the medical needs of children. She purposely didn't mention her connection to him on her resume because she wasn't looking to ride on his coattails. She wanted to secure a position on her own merits.

As the conversation progressed, Lowell appeared to assume the sale. He told Jennifer that they would start her out as a "trainee." They would coach her on passing the Series 7 Exam, paying her a minimal salary of $40,000. Jennifer was well aware that the Series 7 was a grueling six hour exam testing her knowledge of all facets of the stock brokerage industry. The test was a "do or die," situation. Pass, you move on, fail, you're out. Assuming she passes the exam, she would be sent to the "home" office for a two-week training program. Upon her return, she would receive a broker number and begin transacting business. From her understanding, during the first six months she would receive a small salary of $40,000. After that period, she would be on her own earning commissions. Lowell told Jennifer that the average broker at Yardley Tate generates about $700,000 in gross commissions per year, earning $280,000, and has accumulated assets of about a hundred million dollars. With those facts, Jennifer took a deep breath; she always excelled at whatever she set out to accomplish, but attracting $100 million seemed truly intimidating.

It was approaching noontime and Lowell suggested they grab a quick bite at the Bankers Club one floor below. He mentioned that after lunch, she would take a "little psychological exam." He said, "It's no big deal, just standard procedure."

With that he led the way out of his office, past an open trading floor. Jennifer could feel all eyes following her down the hallway. As they left the reception area to the elevators, Lowell made small talk with Jennifer telling her about the history of Tate Yardley. She heard his voice but was too excited to connect with what he was saying. She was thrilled that he invited her to lunch and was envisioning herself entertaining new clients the same way. Jennifer had no idea that he was primarily focused on her two major assets: her beauty and more importantly, the bonus he would receive from her commissions.

As they entered the club, past the Members Only sign, the Maître'D approached Lowell giving him a big handshake and a welcome smile. The room was bustling with waiters carrying big trays and businessmen deep in conversation. They were escorted to a reserved table by the window overlooking the serene Bay. After they were seated, Lowell told Jennifer that the club was known for its Cobb Salad. "But, young lady, make sure you leave room for dessert. Their chocolate chip cookies are made fresh hourly and served warm."

Jennifer took Lowell's advice and ordered the Cobb Salad. When the waiter queried her on her beverage selection, she opted for Pellegrino, "no ice please." She was a little surprised to see Lowell order a "bone dry" martini. She couldn't imagine how he would concentrate on his business after such a strong drink.

Jennifer found Lowell to be quite charming, however throughout their meal, Lowell kept inquiring about Jennifer's family background. She had always been a private person and never liked to discuss her personal life. Lowell was relentless, asking Jennifer how close she was with her famous uncle and if her parents were involved with his business. Frankly, Lowell had a nose for money and sexy women.

After they finished their salads and the table was cleared, the waiter brought over a small platter of the "infamous" chip cookies. Lowell had not steered her wrong, they were warm but crisp on the outside with melted chocolate on the inside. It was a great ending to a delicious meal. After signing for the bill, Lowell said, "OK Ms. Palmer, let's head back to the office and give you the little sales test. I have no doubt you'll pass with flying colors." As they walked out of the club, Lowell slipped his arm around Jennifer's petite waist. Jennifer took notice, but was so eager to fit in, that she pretended to ignore his actions.

When they returned to the office, Jennifer thanked Lowell for lunch. He asked Estelle to set Jennifer up in an empty office so she could take the sales test. Since Jennifer was fresh out of college, another test didn't disturb her. Estelle led Jennifer to a vacated office and closed the door to give her privacy. Jennifer opened the booklet and noticed that the questions were to be answered by a brief response. There were 12 questions. As she read the first question, she thought that this test was some kind of joke. The first question actually read: How would you sell ice to a family of Eskimos? She went on to review the other questions. They appeared to all be equally audacious; if your client refuses to follow your investment recommendation, how would you persuade him to do so? She continued to read on – even if you don't believe in what you are told to sell, how would you convince your client to buy it?

It appeared as though all of the questions either posed scenarios that Jennifer really didn't have any answers for or were out of her frame of reference. Jennifer could feel beads of perspiration developing under her knit dress. The office seemed to be closing in around her. Jennifer responded to the questions as creatively as possible. After reviewing her answers, she steadied herself and stood up, walking out of the office back to Estelle's desk. Reluctantly, she handed the completed test back to the matronly woman. Before she dejectedly turned to leave, Lowell saw Jennifer through his glassed inner sanctum and got up to bid her goodbye. "Jennifer, it was a pleasure to meet you and spend time getting to know you better. I will phone you tomorrow with the results of the test, which I'm sure you aced. We can then move on to plan your future with Tate Yardley."

Jennifer left the office with mixed emotions. On the one hand, she knew that she had made a good impression, but on the other hand, that ridiculous test could be a deal breaker.

That night, Jennifer could barely eat a bite of the meal the housekeeper prepared. Since she felt Jennifer's distress, she had made Cuban comfort food: arroz con pollo with plantains. Unfortunately, Jennifer could barely swallow the tasty meal.

Jennifer was emotionally drained and fraught with anxiety. She knew that if her parents were home, they would tell her that there it made no sense to worry about something that was out of her control. Jennifer knew that she had put her best foot forward at the interview, but also knew that there was no way she could have passed that test. She couldn't sleep a wink that night and was just waiting for tomorrow to arrive.

In contrast to Jennifer, Lowell was having a lovely evening. He felt that he had hit the jackpot with a recruit like Jennifer Palmer; she had all the tools to attract money like flies. Her overwhelming looks and build could melt snow in Alaska.

He assumed that her family's circle of influence was immense. He recalled that Jennifer's uncle had contributed the most dollars to the Robin Hood Foundation, which they had ever received from one donor. Additionally, he had established a charitable remainder trust for the charity to receive upon his death. Lowell knew that with family contacts like that, Jennifer was destined to be a "big producer" in no time. And that meant that he would receive a big upfront bonus for recruiting her and ongoing revenues as she generated commissions. He thought this could be a score for the firm and not bad for the manager.

Before he left the office though, he checked with Estelle to see how Jennifer made out on the test. Estelle looked at Lowell and shook her head. "Lowell, she said, "Jennifer totally flunked the test." Lowell was a bit surprised, but that really didn't matter to him. He wanted Jennifer like a piranha wants meat. He'd report to the home office that she passed with flying colors but intended to give her a hard time for the right to secure a position at Tate Yardley. It even occurred to him that he might get a little action on the side. Jennifer was strikingly beautiful and he knew she wanted the position badly...With that, Lowell was ready to celebrate. He first went back to the Bankers Club for "Happy Hour," with some of the boys from the office and then made plans to take his on again/off again girlfriend to the Forge for a Chateaubriand meal. This was of course, on the corporate expense account. At dinner, he made a toast to himself and his new protégé. Little did Jennifer know what Lowell had in mind for her.

Chapter 8

The next morning, Jennifer thought she heard a phone ringing in her dreams. As she became more awake, she realized that it was 8:00 a.m. and the phone next to her bed was ringing. Groggily, she answered. The voice on the other side said curtly, "Jennifer, this is Estelle from Mr. Abbott's office of Tate Yardley. He would like to meet with you at 2:00 p.m. Please be prompt." Before Jennifer could reply, the woman had hung up. Jennifer felt a shot of adrenaline flow through her body. From the sound of Estelle's voice, Jennifer surmised that something was up. And it didn't sound as though she would be receiving the news she had hoped for. She knew that the results of that test were not good. But wondered how can you determine the value of an individual by evaluating them with one ridiculous test? Plus, she had to be tortured until 2:00 p.m. to find out what her future held at Tate Yardley. Ever since Jennifer was a little girl, she always liked to get the "bad things" over quickly, so she could move on. Well, today she had no choice. Since it was just past eight, she had a chance to take a run and then come home in time to shower and change to be at Tate Yardley on time.

Even though it was already hot outside, the run helped take the edge off Jennifer. It was better than a Valium and gave her a chance to plan her strategy with Lowell. She assumed the worst case scenario of not being offered a position; and planned to defend herself in an intellectual manner. She would use the entire arsenal she had at hand. Lowell appeared to be a nice, savvy businessman, but during their brief time together she garnered that he may not be the sharpest tool in the toolbox. Her plan was to take him out of his comfort zone and debate him with her intellect not her emotions.

Jennifer selected a bright yellow Courreges sheath to wear to the meeting with a strand of black South Seas pearls, along with a tan Hermes Birkin handbag. She knew that looking the part was essential.

Two o'clock couldn't come soon enough. Jennifer was standing at Tate Yardley's reception desk, right on time. She knew that she looked great in her yellow dress and was more than ready for the challenge that awaited her. The receptionist told her that Lowell was just finishing up a meeting, and she would be called in shortly. After about fifteen minutes, Estelle appeared, expressionless as usual, and escorted her back to Abbott's office.

He was on the phone when Jennifer arrived, but motioned for her to sit down. This time, in front of his desk. Jennifer sensed that the games were about to begin. She fostered a forced smile and focused her eyes on his blinking monitor. She observed that the numbers were more green than red, so the market was having a good day, and hopefully, Lowell would be in a good mood.

When he finally got off the phone, he greeted her in a cool but cordial way. He started by saying, "Jennifer, I'm sorry to tell you that the results of the 'psychological sales test,' left much to be desired. Basically, the test results are telling me that you lack any sales ability. As you can imagine, that is a talent that is a prerequisite in this industry. I personally believe that you should seek other opportunities in the business world that are not sales related."

Even though Jennifer had prepared herself for this, actually hearing those words caught her off guard. "Mr. Abbott," she responded, "I respect what you are saying, but it is a bit absurd to ignore the other assets I bring to the table. I am educated, and come from a wonderful family. I have lived and traveled around the world. I speak three languages. How many guys do you have out there working for you that even come close to what I bring to the table? Hire me, I will prove you wrong."

Lowell listened to Jennifer. Sitting back in his chair with his hands clasped behind his head; enjoying the fact that Jennifer Palmer was pleading with him for Job. "Jennifer," he said after a long pause, "we have never hired a woman trainee at Tate Yardley. I would be the first branch manager to do so. I can't afford the risk."

"Lowell, you give me a chance and you will have the opportunity to be one of the most respected managers in the firm. I will make you proud."

Lowell sat up in his chair, appearing to be in deep thought. Finally, what seemed take forever to Jennifer, he said, "Jennifer, look, you are very convincing. I will give you a chance based upon the fact that you meet the following conditions over a specific period of time. To start, you will have only one chance to take and pass the Series 7 exam. We will assist you in studying for the exam in a very limited way. You will be provided with the course material, but after that, you'll be on your own. The exam must be completed within two months of your date of hire. You will be expected to report to the office each day and assist our staff with any special projects they are working on. Once you pass the Series 7, you will be expected to bring in $25 million in customer assets within a three month period. For the first six months of your employment at Tate Yardley you will have a salary of $35,000. Once you are fully licensed and have brought in the $25 million you will be a 100% commission based employee. We will not be sending you to New York for our formal training program. It will be up to you to learn the ropes. I will seat you in an office with a seasoned broker. Hopefully, by spending time with him and hearing how he interacts with his clients, you will develop some sales skills. Jennifer, that's the deal. If you disappoint me, you are out on your ass. There will be no second chances. Have I made myself perfectly clear?"

This was a lot for Jennifer to absorb. But she knew that she had to decide now. This wasn't the time to play games. "Lowell, I appreciate the opportunity that you are extending to me. I accept your offer. You will not be sorry."

"Jennifer," Lowell said, "I'll have a lot riding on your success and expect not to be disappointed." With that, he pressed the intercom and asked Estelle to prepare the employment documents necessary for Jennifer to complete.

"Young lady, I will see you back here tomorrow morning at 8:00 sharp." With that, he got up and shook her hand. "Welcome aboard, Jennifer, now I have to get back to business."

Jennifer walked over to Estelle's desk and ended up spending the next two hours completing employment agreements. In her heart, she knew that she had won this battle. She had succeeded in accomplishing her goal. Now it was up to her to prove her mettle. That, she knew she would do one way or the other.

Chapter 9

The next morning, Jennifer eased her BMW into Tate Yardley's garage. After a victorious conclusion to yesterday's battle and a good night's sleep, Jennifer was eager to get to work. She recalled the same feeling she had on the first day of school after summer break.

Wearing her newly issued ID badge, she proudly strode into Tate Yardley, greeting the receptionist along the way into the main office. She could feel the anticipation in the room for the 9:30 a.m. market opening. Brokers were at their desks, checking their computer monitors, reading the *Wall Street Journal* or on the phone speaking with clients. She did notice a few walking around the office with their coffee eager to engage in conversation. Except for the sales assistants, Jennifer noticed that she was the only woman on the floor.

She approached Estelle's desk to find out what her schedule was for the day. While waiting for Estelle to complete her phone conversation, she looked over at Lowell's glass encased sanctum. His back was to her, but she could see that he was carefully reviewing lines of figures on his computer.

Estelle finished her conversation, got up from her desk and motioned for Jennifer to follow her. They walked to the back of the massive floor to a windowless office the size of a broom closet. Estelle finally uttered her first words of the morning to Jennifer. "This will be your office for the next three months. When you complete your assigned tasks, this is where you will study the course material I gave to you yesterday." Jennifer looked at the small office with its bold fluorescent lighting. She was obviously disappointed with her new quarters, but assumed it would only be for a temporary basis.

"Jennifer, leave your purse in here, we have things to do." With that, Estelle led Jennifer to a large room, full of built-in floor to ceiling file drawers. In the center of the room was a rolling file drawer chock full of papers. Without any eye contact, Estelle said to Jennifer, "These are monthly annuity statements for the entire branch; they need to be filed in the drawers on the wall. As you place the most recent file in each client's folder, please take out the previous month's statement. When you complete this task, you will take all of the old statements to the shredder. Any questions?"

Jennifer shook her head. As Estelle left the room, Jennifer thought that she definitely wasn't cut out for menial labor. But, on the other hand was smart enough to realize that this was merely a means to an end.

Jennifer spent the next three months completing similar assignments. She would grab whatever spare time she had, either in or out of the office, to study her course material.

She was the only "trainee" in the office and aside from the typical curiosity of finding out who this beautiful woman was, her presence was generally ignored by the other brokers. A few of the sales assistants would offer her a kind word every so often and invite her to join them for lunch. Jennifer would gracefully decline their invitations to take advantage of any free time to study. On occasion, Lowell would come by, always reminding her that the clock was ticking and "his ass was on the line." She so appreciated his reassuring words.

Two weeks before her exam date, she decided that it would be prudent to invest in the Series 7 "crash course." This was a two week course that was in session for nine hours a day. She had heard that this course produced an 85% passing rate. She knew that the firm would not invest another penny in her, but hoped they would allow her to take off the time. Grudgingly, Lowell acquiesced, with the parting words of, "Jennifer, even though you're paying for the course, you are still earning a salary from us. Make it work."

She wondered if he was this belligerent with the other brokers, but knew that she would soon find out.

The "crash course" came and went. Even though it proved to be an arduous two week experience, Jennifer felt that it was worth her investment. By passing the final exam, she felt the confidence necessary for the Series 7.

The day of the dreaded six hour exam finally arrived. The weather was appropriately bleak and rainy. As it turned out, Jennifer didn't need the full six hours to complete the test. She felt very well prepared after having taken the prep "crash course" and felt that she had passed the exam. When she handed the proctor her final answers, she lifted the pages to her lips for a quick good luck kiss. As she walked back to her car, she felt as though a two ton weight had been lifted from her shoulders. Unfortunately though, she wouldn't have a clue as to the results for at least two more weeks. She really was in the mood to celebrate the fact that the tortuous studying had come to an end, but was reluctant to do so until she knew the positive results.

The subsequent two weeks were like a sentence. Since she still wasn't licensed and could not conduct or solicit business, all she could do at the office was busywork. And apparently, Estelle was able to provide her with a constant flow. She noticed that Lowell totally ignored her. He never even asked her how the test was. Jennifer desperately needed a vacation, but knew that this was not the time to request time off.

The days passed too slowly for Jennifer. Her patience level was starting to wear thin. Two weeks to the day that she took the Series 7, she decided to treat herself to a mani/pedi during her lunch hour. As the manicurist was brushing the top coat on her freshly painted hot coral colored toes, Jennifer's cell phone rang. Jennifer really didn't want to answer it. She much preferred to luxuriate in the moment. However, something prompted her to dig into the depths of her Vuitton bag and respond to the rings. Before Jennifer could say hello, she heard Estelle's monotone voice, "Jennifer, Mr. Abbott would like to see you now. Be here in fifteen minutes." With that, Jennifer heard the dial tone. Her intuition told her that the exam results must be posted and it was Lowell who was going to give her the news. At least now, she would learn the outcome of all her hard work.

Needless to say, the absolute embarrassment and ramifications of failing would be devastating to Jennifer. She gathered her things and with freshly painted toe nails raced out of the salon, down the street, back to the office. Before she knew it, the elevator had reached the penthouse floor. This might be her last ride up to Tate Yardley.

Even though she had a pit in the base of her stomach, Jennifer was a good actress, so she appeared to confidently stride past the reception desk and through the main floor, making a beeline to Lowell's office. She paused at Estelle's desk and was told by the "dragon lady," "he's been waiting for you." When she walked into Lowell's office he appeared to be deep in thought, his back to her, looking at his computer monitor.

Jennifer broke the silence. "Lowell, you asked to see me?"

Abruptly, Lowell turned his chair around to face Jennifer. He appeared stone-faced. Jennifer had an inkling that this wasn't going to be good.

He had a folder on his desk; she could see her name on it. He started by saying, "Jennifer, we received your Series 7 exam results this afternoon. As I told you during your initial interview, passing this test was the first bogey you needed to accomplish to secure a position at Tate Yardley."

Jennifer searched his face for an indication of where this conversation might lead. But he maintained the look of an experienced poker player. He continued, "Jennifer, I know that the past three months haven't been easy for you. It was probably excruciating at times." As he continued to speak, he slowly rose out of his chair, extending his hand. "Jennifer, I am pleased to tell you that you passed the Series 7 exam. Welcome Aboard."

After hearing those words, "you passed," Jennifer felt an immediate elation. She was absolutely ecstatic. The feeling of accomplishment was so overwhelming that she felt tears of joy come to her eyes, but she quickly composed herself. Lowell came around the front of his desk to where Jennifer was sitting and gave her a hug and kiss on the cheek. "Jennifer, I'm proud of you, now let's see what kind of broker you can be. Estelle has already received your broker number, I believe it's 22. Tomorrow you will be moving in with George Jenkins. He's an old-timer and has kindly volunteered to show you the ropes. George has been with the firm for over 40 years. By sharing an office with him, you will hear how he transacts business with his clients and garner the product knowledge you need to move forward. Within 48 hours, you will officially be licensed to conduct and solicit business. In the meantime, why don't you take the rest of the afternoon off? Tomorrow morning, I expect to see you at the 8:30 a.m. sales meeting."

As Jennifer left Lowell's office, he was thinking about how right he had played her. Freezing her out for the past several months just made her wanting to work Tate Yardley that much more. And he loved seeing her squirm before he revealed the exam results. Lowell knew that he had the ace of diamonds in his pocket. Between her family's wealth and her circle of friends, he could see her becoming a million dollar producer in no time. Now that she would be licensed and going into production, Lowell was secured of receiving the first tranche of his "recruiting bonus." Jennifer was going to be his lottery ticket, and Lowell would make sure that the ticket paid off big.

Jennifer practically flew out of Lowell's office. As she passed Estelle's desk, the only comment the woman could muster was, "Jennifer, your attendance at tomorrow morning's sales meeting is mandatory." Jennifer was so elated that even Estelle's bitter attitude couldn't faze her.

Jennifer took the elevator down to the garage level. As the doors opened, she rushed to her car. She couldn't wait to call her parents and tell them the news. After dialing their number, her mother answered the phone. "Mom. I passed the test! I can't believe it! I am so excited!"

Her mother pretended to share in her daughter's happiness, but secretly had been hoping that this whole stock brokerage idea would fizzle out. She could not imagine her daughter in a sales career. It just wasn't the Palmer way...Still, she knew that she had to support her daughter and share in her happiness. "Jennifer, your father and I are so proud of you. We just knew that you would pass that test with flying colors. Come home and let's celebrate. I'll make reservations at Chez Maurice for this evening. I'll speak to the chef and make sure he makes the Dover Sole Almandine that I know you love."

Since Jennifer's break-up with Brook, she hadn't had a favorite man in her life. Over the past couple of years, she had certainly dated her share of losers. She longed for a soul mate with whom she could share happy times such as this. But, she thought, she was on the brink of a whole new life, who knew what could be waiting for her on the horizon. Now she would have a better opportunity to mingle and network with quality clients. She might even meet a nice broker in the office.

With that thought, Jennifer reached up in the car and pressed the button to lower the convertible top. The fresh air surrounded her, blowing her blond hair in the wind. She stepped on the gas, turned the volume of her CD player on high, and flew down the garage exit to the freeway entrance. Jennifer knew that she was on her way, with a firm grasp on her future. She was finally in control of her own destiny.

Chapter 10

After an evening of jubilant celebration, a little Veuve Clicquot and scrumptious French cuisine, Jennifer's excitement carried over to the next morning. She woke up early enough to fit in a four mile run. It was the first day of October and the humid air was showing signs of lifting. As she jogged home Jennifer looked up at the sky and saw the graceful flocks of white egrets heading toward the sunrise.

Jennifer wore a light pink Chanel suit with matching slingbacks. She wanted to make a statement at her first sales meeting: Jennifer Palmer was a force to be reckoned with.

She made it to the office in half an hour with fifteen minutes to spare before the start of the meeting.

The sales meetings were always off limits to the support staff and "trainees." Only the brokers were permitted to attend. Jennifer was quite curious to finally find out what took place behind those closed doors. Since this was her first meeting, she decided to enter the conference room early and secure a front row seat. The room was large, with desks lined up facing the front where a podium stood in front of a large white presentation board, with colored markers and an eraser.

Jennifer took out a new leather bound notepad and Montblanc pen out of her orange Hermes briefcase. She pretended to be writing notes as the other brokers began to amble in. Adjacent to the conference room was an adequate kitchen with a table set up with bagels, cream cheese and glazed doughnuts. On their way in, most of the brokers detoured into the kitchen, helping themselves to the food.

This was the first time Jennifer had seen all the brokers in the office assembled in one room. Most of them she noticed, could afford to skip the breakfast selections. They were all shapes and sizes. Most were in their forties and out of shape. Jennifer noticed that one broker was so fat, that he looked as though he were carrying twins. The preponderance of the men was attired in a white shirt and colorful tie. A few were more informal, wearing polo shirts and khaki pants. One broker in particular stood out to Jennifer. He looked like a walking designer logo. With his Hermes tie and belt, Ferragamo loafers, Hilditch and Key shirt and to top the ensemble, a Breguet watch. Even Jennifer, who enjoyed quality clothing thought he was a little over the top for a guy. But she also knew that these were to be her colleagues and it was inappropriate to jump to any judgment. She was looking forward to working with them and assumed that it would be a team effort.

The room was filling up. Even though most of the seats were taken, Jennifer noticed that no one claimed the chair next to her. She felt that she was still a novelty to this group and they were steering clear of her. She did notice though, lots of side glances her way. Just before the meeting began, "Mr. Designer Logo," boldly took the seat next to Jennifer. He introduced himself as Lawrence and asked her for her name as well. As she began to introduce herself, Lowell walked to the front of the room. "Gentleman and lady, I'd like your attention." The room became silent. Lowell walked over to the white board and picked up a blue marker, writing in capital letters: POSOM. After reading that word, Jennifer was perplexed. She knew that she was attending a stock brokerage sales meeting not a biology class (with a misspelled word).

Lowell again started speaking. "OK guys, last month was good for the branch, but not good enough. Year over year we're only up 10%. We are averaging an annualized gross total for the year of $20 million. That is unsatisfactory. Our year-end goal is $25 million and it's up to each one of you to get your numbers up. If you each did an extra $10,000 per month through the end of the year, we will achieve our goal. With that in mind, I'd like you all to focus on this month's POSOM. It's an income oriented closed end fund that will put 3% in your pocket. I expect each of you to ticket a minimum of 25,000 shares. No ifs, ands or buts about it. You help me attain our goal and I'll make sure you have access to the hottest IPOs plus throw a celebratory year-end party at the best restaurant in town. Am I understood? Now go, let's do some business."

In unison, the brokers got up to head back to their offices. Lawrence was walking with Jennifer. "Hey, I didn't get your name."

Jennifer turned to him and introduced herself, adding, "What did he mean by POSOM?"

"Within days, I'm sure you'll figure it out on your own. By the way, I see we both like Hermes." Looking at him, Jennifer didn't know whether to interpret his remark as a compliment or insult. Lawrence kept walking alongside her as she was heading to her new quarters. "Jennifer, how about joining me for lunch today?"

Jennifer looked at him and smiled sweetly, saying, "Lawrence, since I'm the rookie here, I think it's better if I work through lunch, at least for the next few weeks. But thanks for the offer."

Jennifer had no desire to have lunch with Lawrence or anyone else in the office for that matter. She was here to work, not make new friends. She knew that these were her colleagues and didn't want to take it further than that. This was a wonderful opportunity for her and she planned to take full advantage of it.

"OK," Lawrence said, "I'll give you a rain check." Jennifer could hardly wait.

An extra desk had been set up in George Jenkins' office. As she walked in, she saw a slim, older gentleman, with slightly balding gray hair. He was sitting directly behind the desk that she assumed was hers. He was wearing a crisp white shirt with a simple red tie. Over his shirt was a light blue cardigan.

As he looked up from his work, he noticed Jennifer enter the room. He immediately extended his hand to Jennifer with a warm smile. "I understand you're my new rookie, I'm George Jenkins." Jennifer was surprised that he didn't get up, but then suddenly realized that he was sitting in a wheelchair. "Mr. Jenkins, it's a pleasure to meet you."

He immediately interrupted her, "Jennifer, please call me George. Lowell has told me a little bit about you. I will make every effort to help you in any way I possibly can. This is a tough business and with the way the world is these days, only getting tougher. But, I tell you, if you do right by your clients, they'll stick with you through thick and thin. Treat their money as though it's yours and you will be assured of a successful career. Now, the market is just about to open and I need to get in touch with a couple of my clients. From what I understand, Estelle has a new broker package for you. I'm sure she'll walk you through it." He was interrupted by the ringing phone. "Jennifer, the first lesson I can teach you," he said, as he reached for the phone, "is don't let your phone ring more than twice. Service is the name of the game. Please excuse me." With that, George answered the phone. "George here, how can I help you?"

Jennifer felt a bit awkward eavesdropping on his conversation, so she got up and decided it was time to tackle Estelle. As Jennifer approached, Estelle, who was as usual on the phone, glanced up at her from her desk without acknowledging her presence. When the woman finally hung up the phone, Jennifer in an effort to be nice, began, "Estelle, how are you today?"

Estelle ignored her query and handed Jennifer the package. "Go back to your office, log onto your computer, create a password and follow the instructions in the package. You must complete this enrollment today in order to receive the employee benefits. If you have questions, call Human Resources. Once you finish your benefits enrollment, you will spend the rest of your time cold calling this list of prospects. The names and numbers are 'clean,' so you should have no solicitation issues. All of your free time will be dedicated to cold calling the names on that list."

Estelle abruptly turned her back on Jennifer and began a conversation with the assistant at the adjacent desk. Jennifer took this as a signal of dismissal. Jennifer walked back to her office with the package and a huge printout of prospect names and numbers. She thought that this was the longest conversation she'd had thus far with Estelle and no matter what, and as difficult as it was, she had to stay on her good side. That is, if she even had a good side.

Back at the office, Jennifer was able to log onto the computer and proceed to enroll in the benefits programs. All the while, she was listening to George's conversations with his clients. She was impressed by the consideration and patience he displayed to his clients. She was looking forward to engaging with her own future clients in the same fashion. He really seemed to be the perfect prototype of the ideal stockbroker.

Jennifer now had the onerous task of cold calling the list of prospects that Estelle had given to her. She perused the list of thousands of names. Along with the list came a script detailing exactly what to say to the strangers on the other side of the phone. The product she was to pitch was the fund Lowell was pushing at the morning's sales meeting. At the bottom of the script in big bold print was: SALES CHARGE=3.00% IN YOUR POCKET. This was going to be an impossible task. Jennifer couldn't imagine calling complete strangers and attempt to sell them an investment product that may or may not suit their financial needs.

She turned around and asked George what the 3% sales charge meant? "Jennifer, that's the amount you will get paid based on how much the client invests. For example, if they invest $10,000, you will receive a gross commission of $300, of that amount; your net portion would be about $100. The balance goes to the firm. Some of the brokers in the office just focus on those types of products because of the high sales charge. Typically, they'll have the client hold the product for a minimal period of time and then have them sell it, generating still another commission. Lowell was pushing it at the meeting this morning because the branch stands to make a killing with these kinds of products. The more the branch generate the bigger his bonus will be. It's as simple as that."

Jennifer was surprised at how more emphasis was placed on the commissions produced than on what was really right for the client. "George," Jennifer asked, "so why did he have the word POSOM written on the board this morning?"

George gave her a sheepish grin. "You don't know what that stands for?"

Jennifer said, "I thought it had something to do with an animal. I really couldn't figure it out."

"Well my dear," George said, "welcome to the cold, calculating world of investing other people's money. Please excuse my language, but it stands for: 'Piece of Shit of the Month.' We all have to sell some of it. Around here it's all about politics. If you make the management look good, you'll be taken care of. Go against the system and you're doomed."

Needless to say, Jennifer was aghast. "You're pulling my leg aren't you, George?"

George smiled. "I wish I were, my dear. But you have to start somewhere, so you might as well begin with selling that product. Just don't put too much in any one client's portfolio. You definitely don't want to create a concentrated position in junk like that."

The second page of the product profile had a written script with Q's and A's, addressing all possible prospect queries. Jennifer never imagined that this was the prescribed way to attract new clients. She took a deep breath and braced up for the task at hand.

By 3:30, she had made over 60 calls. At least 75% of the respondents hung up on her, a few who just seemed plain lonely welcomed a voice on the other side of the phone and the rest were just plain rude, cursing her with expletives, before hanging up. Just about at the same time, she noticed Lowell walking around the office. He was clapping his hands and stopping by each broker's office shouting, "A half hour left to get your orders in. Let's make it a big production day! Get those orders in now."

Jennifer thought he looked like a barker at a carnival. She couldn't believe that he was pushing the brokers to get orders in before the close. This environment was definitely not what she had expected from a sterling wire house. She recalled her early experience with her dad's broker. It never was like this. She assumed that her father's financial welfare was far more important to his broker than generating commissions. At least that was the illusion that was created.

With each passing day, the call list became more and more onerous to Jennifer. After a two week period of cold calling, Jennifer only opened up two accounts.

One account was for an elderly couple who agreed to invest $20,000. After speaking with them at length and answering every conceivable question, she actually felt guilty about taking their money to invest in such a questionable product. The other account was for a widow who had been left an estate by her husband. She had alluded to the fact that it was a sizeable estate, but agreed to open an account for only $10,000. Jennifer felt that once the lady got to know her better, she would invest more.

To add insult to injury, Lawrence would stop by the office on a regular basis to check up on Jennifer. He would always let her know how much "gross" he had produced that day. Apparently, from what he said, he had placed over 100,000 shares in the POSOM. Jennifer figured that the guy just didn't have a conscience. But on the other hand, she assumed that he was probably one of the more favored brokers in the office and got whatever favors he asked for.

Jennifer also noticed that every morning before the market opened, there was a list posted in the center of the office, showing what each broker had made in revenues the prior day, as well as what their rank in the office was for the month and the year. Lawrence's name always appeared in the top five. Of course, her numbers were so dismal that her name always appeared at the end of the list. Jennifer had always excelled at whatever she did and now just because she had a high ethical standard, and was new to this industry she was humiliated on a daily basis. Maybe her parents had been right and she had selected a career that was not for her. Only time would tell.

Chapter 11

On the last day of the month, the charming Estelle stopped by Jennifer's desk saying, "Lowell would like to see you at 1:00." It was only 8:30, and Jennifer had to wait almost five hours to find out what was on Lowell's mind. She assumed that this was his little power play. He reminded her of the diminutive French emperor of fame.

At 1:00 exactly, Jennifer walked back to Lowell's office. He motioned for her to enter, but did not offer her a seat. Jennifer took one anyway.

He began, "Jennifer, if you recall, when I agreed to hire you, we had a deal. First, you had to pass the Series 7 exam, which you did. The second condition was that you bring in $20 million dollars in assets over the three month period beginning from the day you are officially licensed. Today is the end of month one. You have opened a total of three accounts with assets totaling $225,000. I noticed that one of the three accounts is your own. So net-net, you've opened two accounts in the last month. Plus, you have generated gross of $750. To me these results are deplorable. Are you aware that the average broker in this office generates over $70,000 of commissions a month?

I know that you are a new recruit, so let's ignore the commissions for a moment; instead let's focus on the assets. Jennifer, we both know you come from a wealthy background, at the very least, you should have your parents and other family members open up accounts with you. They need to support you. Come on, Jennifer, I had high hopes for you and I'm sorry to say you have disappointed me. Look, you have two months left to achieve your goals. I want to see your name move toward the top of the daily commission roster. If not, I'll have no other option but to let you go. You're a smart girl; I know you'll figure it out, one way or the other." With that final statement, he waved her out of the office.

Jennifer walked out totally pissed. She had only been licensed for a month and Lowell was readying the guillotine for her demise. He definitely reminded her of a little Napoleon who enjoyed the art of intimidation.

She dejectedly walked back to her office. George immediately noticed an anguished look on Jennifer's face. He could tell that she was distressed about something. "Jennifer, what happened? Where's that pretty smile I'm used to seeing?"

Jennifer replied, "I've just been given an ultimatum from Lowell. If I don't open more accounts and generate more business in the next two months, I'm out of here. I'm not a magician, George. It is soooo difficult to cold call. I just despise doing it."

"Look, Jennifer," George said, "just like you hear me interacting on the phone with my clients, I hear you cold calling. You don't come across with any conviction. You are losing your audience basically after your introduction. I have a suggestion for you. Instead of cold calling that list of names, why don't you start mailing out written solicitations? Come up with a catchy short letter that will motivate the recipient to pick up the phone and call you. This way, you can set up an appointment; have them come to the office and meet you. Once you've got them in the door, with a little of my coaching, you'll have them eating out of your hand."

Jennifer appreciated George's input thought it was a great idea and went right to work at composing a letter. By the next morning, she had come up with a four line letter with an action ending. She showed it to George, who gave her the go ahead and then proceeded to secure the necessary approvals to expedite the mailing. Since she didn't use a pre-approved form letter and opted for ingenuity, Jennifer had to practically jump through hoops to defend her letter. Of course, Lowell thought it was a bad idea, but with her coaxing agreed to let the letter go out with a few changes made by the regional complex compliance officer. This experience showed her exactly what it takes to get anything through the system. Jennifer came to find out that the "compliance officer" was really a Gestapo agent re-incarnated. The woman kept insisting to Jennifer that she was just trying to protect her, and not trying to give her a hard time. Jennifer translated that to mean, that she could really care less about Jennifer but was just looking to protect Tate Yardley.

Finally, with the "official" go-ahead to move forward, Jennifer stuffed and addressed the letters. Included in the mailing was a tear sheet for the prospect to complete with their name, phone number, address and their area of investment interest. Included with the letter was a pre-paid return envelope on which Jennifer wrote her name. She sent out 1,000 letters and then impatiently waited for the responses to come in. Each afternoon Jennifer would head to the mailroom to find out if any replies had come in for her. As the days passed, she spent more time absorbing George's style with his clients. She wanted to pick up as much information as possible from him so she would be ready to handle her own clientele. There was a lot to learn and she felt fortunate to have been assigned to him. George was an honest, hardworking man with a good heart. Jennifer was still at the cold calling but was also beginning to develop her own point of view. An investment philosophy that was solid and could easily be shared with new prospects.

Within two weeks, eight return envelopes showed up. Unfortunately, five of them were returned because of undeliverable addresses, but three appeared to be real responses. One was from a small Mom and Pop apparel company. They were only interested in a place to park their working capital. But still, Jennifer reasoned, opening an account with them would add to her asset base. They deposited $200,000 into the money market account.

The second response was from a middle-aged widow. Jennifer met with her in the office's conference room. Lenore Roberts was an attractive woman. She was about 5'6" with platinum blonde hair, pulled back in a tight chignon at the nape of her neck. Jennifer surmised that she had gone under the knife because she didn't have a wrinkle on her face. She was dressed smartly in a beige Calvin Klein sheath dress accessorized with a coin necklace, bronze mules and a gold threaded cardigan draped casually around her neck.

Instantly, Jennifer felt the chemistry with Lenore and more importantly, she knew she could help her. Lenore told her how she had gone through a series of brokers, all male as it turned out. Her $2 million inheritance was now worth $1.5 million and Lenore could not afford to lose any more money. She told Jennifer that when she received her note, she was so happy to be contacted by a woman broker. The others never took the time to explain anything to her. She felt as though she had been financially raped by them. She needed help. Jennifer assured Lenore that no transactions would take place without her full understanding. First, Jennifer had to find out from Lenore what her expenses were and how much income she was bringing in aside from the account. After meeting for over an hour, Lenore felt comfortable enough with Jennifer to sign the papers to electronically wire her account in to Tate Yardley from the brokerage firm where it previously was invested.

Lenore didn't want to call her former broker and get into a confrontational situation. Jennifer assured her that wasn't necessary and everything would be transferred to Tate Yardley within five business days. Lenore was so pleased with their meeting that she gave Jennifer a hug as they walked to the elevator. For the first time, Jennifer felt like a real broker. She opened a sizeable account and was actually helping someone improve their financial life. She thought, wasn't that the way this business is supposed to be?

The third response that had come in that week was from an A. Smith. They had written their phone number and address on the tear sheet and indicated that they were interested in municipal bonds. Jennifer noticed that their address was located in one of the most affluent areas of Coral Gables. The community called, "Gables Estates." She had gone to school with several classmates who lived there, so she was quite familiar with the neighborhood. The price of a home there started at $5 million and went up to over $20 million. Knowing what she knew about the area, Jennifer was trembling as she dialed the number. A man answered the phone. "Mr. Smith," she began, "this is Jennifer Palmer from Tate Yardley. I recently received a response from you regarding your interest in municipal bonds. How may I help you?"

The man on the other end of the phone had a nice voice. "Jennifer, your note intrigued me. I have $10 million to invest and as you saw from my response, am particularly interested in tax-frees. When can we get together?"

Jennifer, attempting to cover her excitement said as coolly as possible, "Well Mr. Smith, our offices are located on Brickell Avenue. When would it be convenient for you to make an appointment?"

"Jennifer, I would prefer that you come to the house. I'm a busy man and don't have the time to drive downtown."

A little frustrated, Jennifer tried again, "Mr. Smith, I can meet with you anytime here in the office."

Mr. Smith firmly replied, "Jennifer, I would prefer that you come here. Right now it's 11:00 a.m., why don't you come by at 2:00? Do you know where I am located?" Smith proceeded to give her directions, ending with, "I'll leave your name at the gate."

By the time Jennifer hung up the phone, George could sense her exuberance. She immediately turned around to George and said, "George, I think this last call will launch my career. The man who responded to my note wants to meet with me right away. The only thing is, he wants me to go to his house. Isn't that a bit odd?"

"Look Jennifer, make sure you give me his number so we know where you are. But honestly, between you and me, your back is up against a wall here, you really have no choice but to go over there. I've met with lots of clients at their homes, it's no big deal. The likelihood of anything happening is remote. And like you said, opening up a large account like that would definitely jumpstart your career. You know, it's all black and white here. You either bring in assets and generate revenues, or you're the low man on the totem pole. And around here, they won't let you forget that. Remember to take all the new account paperwork with you. Make sure he signs and dates everything. You don't want to drive back there. Jennifer, you'll be fine. I have a lot of faith in you."

Jennifer was simultaneously ecstatic and apprehensive. She never thought that the job of a stockbroker would entail house calls. Physicians didn't even make them anymore. But right now, she needed Mr. Smith a whole lot more than he needed her.

She spent the next two hours assembling the paperwork and reviewing the information she had previously learned about municipal bonds. George helped her print out a list of existing inventory, so she would be able to give Mr. Smith an idea of what was available in the marketplace.

At 1:15 she pulled out of the garage and sped off toward the private enclave of Gables Estates. She had gotten dressed that morning for a day of regular office work. At the time, she didn't have a clue that she would be possibly meeting her biggest client. She was wearing a short sleeved cashmere pink top with a white St. John skirt. A string of simple white pearls and her standard Ferragamo bowed flats completed the ensemble. Maybe it was better that she wasn't over-dressed. This was a client meeting after all, not a date. Maybe, one of the most important meetings in her life.

By the time Jennifer steered the car through the guard gate at Gables Estates, she was practically hyperventilating. Mr. Smith's directions were perfect. The house was located right around the first bend. Jennifer recalled passing it dozens of times on her social visits to the neighborhood with her former classmates. It had the appearance of a small French chateau hidden and protected by ten foot ficus hedges. The grounds were meticulously manicured with beautiful topiaries surrounding the house. There were double garages on each side with a fountain at the center of the circular gravel driveway. As Jennifer got out of the car, she noticed Koi fish swimming in the pool of the fountain. She picked up her briefcase, took a deep breath and headed toward the front door. As she rang the bell, she heard dogs barking and the sound of footsteps approaching the door.

The door was opened by a portly man with a ruddy complexion. His features were non-descript, except for the fact that he was unshaven. His eyes were brown and heavily bloodshot. He looked like he hadn't taken a shower in days. He was wearing a black and white stripped silk shirt with its tails hanging over a faded pair of jeans. Jennifer noticed that he was barefoot. Beside him were two barking Rottweilers with heavy choke chains. "You must be Jennifer, wait here while I put, the boys away." While she waited outside the door, Jennifer peered into the house. She saw polished white marble flooring but little else. The house looked empty. Maybe she thought, he was just moving in.

A minute later, Mr. Smith reappeared. "Jennifer, please follow me to my office. As they walked through the house to his office, the only furnishings that Jennifer saw were two unmade cots in what she supposed to be the living room. She thought it was a little strange, but quickly dismissed the lack of furnishings from her mind. She was there to open a new account not to assist him with his interior design. Mr. Smith's office was a sharp contrast to the starkness of the rest of the house. There was a big glass desk, piled high with papers. A half eaten sub sandwich was lying beside the paperwork. Facing the desk, mounted on the ceiling were four flat screen monitors, all blinking away with some sort of trading activity. One wall was lined with a bookcase and the other with an aquarium backlit in neon blue, containing about thirty multi-colored tropical fish. Mr. Smith sat down behind his desk in an over-sized leather chair on rollers. He gestured for Jennifer to take a seat on the upholstered chair facing his desk.

Before she had a chance to say a word, Mr. Smith initiated the conversation. "Jennifer, as we discussed on the phone, I'd like to open an account with you today. Deposit $10 million and purchase only AAA municipal bonds."

While he spoke, his eyes kept glancing up at the monitors. He continued, "Just make sure that the money is liquid in case I need cash on short notice. So what do we need to do to expedite my request?"

Jennifer replied, "Mr. Smith, I brought a list of what we currently have available in our inventory."

"Jennifer," Smith interrupted, "just find me AAA tax-frees that I can have access to if necessary. I don't need to look over your inventory."

Needless to say, Jennifer was a bit uncomfortable with his approach, but pulled out the new account paperwork for him to complete. While she was compiling the applications, she was wondering to herself why he had come to her. He was obviously a sophisticated investor with all those monitors. Maybe, she reasoned, he just needed assistance with fixed income. And, of course, she was more than willing to help. Earlier, back at the office, George had given her a checklist of questions that needed to be answered for an account opening. She could sense by Smith's tone that this was going to be a challenge.

Jennifer replied to Mr. Smith, "It would be my pleasure to assist you with your investments. Before we open your account, is there anything you would like to ask me about my background?"

"Not really," he said, "let's just get the account opened. I'm sure you have the credentials to purchase tax-free bonds for me. So, tell me what you need."

Jennifer started with the standard questions, including name, address, social security number, net worth, etc. When she asked him what his annual income was, Mr. Smith asked, "Why in the hell do you need to know that?" She patiently explained to him that these questions needed to be answered in order to establish his suitability as a client to invest in munis.

He countered with, "I'm giving you a check for $10 million, which should be enough suitability to answer all your questions."

Jennifer tried to placate him in the best way she knew possible. "Mr. Smith, this is protocol, all the information you are revealing to me is 100% confidential. There aren't many more questions to answer. I'll make this as painless as possible for you. In fact, we're just about finished."

Suddenly, the phone rang. Mr. Smith immediately answered it, got up and indicated that he had to take the call in another room. As he walked out, Jennifer heard him switch to Spanish. Since French was her first language, she was able to pick up a few words from the conversation as he walked away. She heard something about a delivery from Cali. And she also heard 100 million dineros, along with "rapido." Maybe, she thought he was in the floral business. After all, the majority of flowers sold in the United States come from Colombia.

When he walked out of the room, he had left the door slightly ajar. As she was completing the account paperwork, she heard sounds coming from a nearby room. Apparently, Mr. Smith had taken his call in another room a distance away from his office. Jennifer was curious as to where the sounds were coming from. She put her papers down on the chair next to her, standing up and walking to the open doorway. Immediately across from the office was what appeared to be the kitchen? She heard voices coming from there. As she looked into the kitchen, she saw several young men with their backs to her. They were wearing camouflage-like attire and looked like terrorists Jennifer had seen on TV. They appeared out of shape and unshaven. Some had long stringy hair with heavy beards. They were drinking bottles of Corona beer, speaking Spanish and appeared to be having a good time. Jennifer was not prepared for what she saw next. Lying on the granite counter top of the center island was a mound of automatic guns and rifles. As she absorbed what she was looking at, she heard footsteps heading her way. It must be Smith. She didn't want him to see what she had uncovered. She quickly went back to her seat. When he came back into the room he said, "Sorry for the interruption, now let's get back to the paperwork."

Jennifer knew that she had to gracefully exit the scene in a way that he wouldn't have a clue as to what she had just seen. She quickly started putting the papers back in her briefcase, standing up at the same time. "Mr. Smith, I'm two months pregnant and still having morning sickness. I just felt a wave of nausea and would hate to throw up on your beautiful oriental rug. I'll be in touch with you." Before he had a chance to speak, she rushed out of the office down the corridor to the front door. Yanking it open and slamming it shut, she ran out to her car. Her car keys had fallen into the depths of her briefcase. Shaking like a leaf, she finally located the keys, opened the door, and threw her briefcase in the passenger seat. Jennifer couldn't start the ignition fast enough, skidding out the gravel driveway.

After seeing those terrorist looking men with their guns she had become petrified. Mr. Smith must be a major Colombian drug lord looking for a way to launder his money. He had selected the perfect pawn in Jennifer. If she hadn't seen the goons with their guns, she definitely would have conducted business with him.

It took her several minutes to collect herself. Her adrenaline was pumping so hard that she couldn't stop perspiring. She wanted to pull over and just strip off her sweater. Instead, she put the A/C on high and tried to cool down. Jennifer was literally in a state of shock. If they knew what she had seen, she probably wouldn't have made it out of that house alive. As she started to calm down and gather her wits, she was relieved to be out of there, but also disappointed that she hadn't landed the big "elephant."

How could her instincts have led her so awry? Obviously, she was so desperate to open an account that she didn't even think to follow her instincts. In retrospect, Mr. Smith or whatever his name was had been determined to open an account with her. Apparently he was on the prowl for a novice who would do whatever necessary to land a $10 million account.

Jennifer was emotionally and mentally spent. She decided to go directly home, rather than back to the office. The firm knew she was out on an appointment and it was almost 4:00, surely she wouldn't be missed. Even though she wasn't planning on returning to the office today, she knew that eventually she would have to face the wrath of Lowell.

As soon as she got home, Jennifer stripped off her clothes and made a mad dash to the shower. She couldn't wait to cleanse her body of what she had just experienced. Feeling the spray of warm water hitting her head began to slowly relax her. She turned on the steam and slowly inhaled the eucalyptus scent. The warm heat enveloped the core of her soul. She finally felt safe.

Coming out of the steam shower, she wrapped a plush terry towel around her body. Without even bothering to put on a robe, she walked downstairs to the bar and poured herself a double scotch. Jennifer wasn't a big drinker, but relished the first swallow of the golden elixir. She could feel her anxiety floating away. Thank God, Mr. Smith didn't have her home address or phone number. She had used her wits to get out of there. She wanted to call the police and let them know what was going on in that house, but thought better of it. It wasn't worth taking a chance. These were bad people. She had learned her lesson. Neither Lowell, Tate Yardley or anyone else would ever force her to put her life in danger to acquire an account. Jennifer took another sip of the scotch and looked forward to a great dinner with her parents and a good night's sleep.

Chapter 12

After a fitful, Ambien assisted night's sleep; Jennifer groggily got up to face the day. She could still feel that her body was in an anxiety mode since her previous day's experience. At dinner last night, she didn't even mention a word about it to her parents. She knew that if they knew, they would have insisted on calling the police as well as pressuring her to quit the job that she was trying so hard to preserve.

Doing her best to move forward, Jennifer quickly showered and dressed. While driving to the office, she kept second guessing herself. Maybe this business wasn't for her. While she was still young, maybe she should go back to school and try to again pursue a career in medicine. She knew that if she chose to go back to medical school, at best, it would take 10 to twelve years to even begin to earn a living. She just couldn't picture herself being dependent on her parents for that long. She was looking forward to moving out of the house and becoming an independent young lady. In fact yesterday, before the horrible meeting, she had even fantasized about buying a condo overlooking the bay. She had even thought about how much fun it would be decorate. Well, so much for that. As she drove into the garage, she attempted to give herself a reality check. Despite yesterday, she knew that she had to be more positive. She had to give this career a chance. After all, she had fought so hard to get in.

When Jennifer entered the office, George had been expectantly awaiting her arrival. He immediately could tell by the look on Jennifer's face that the outcome of yesterday's meeting was not good. George had been around the block often enough to know the unpredictability of the business. There were so many variables, which were out of your control. Between the clients, firm politics and world events, it was impossible to be in control of your own destiny. By seeing Jennifer's expression, he didn't want to add to her pressure. Instead, he decided to lighten up, complimenting Jennifer on how nice she looked and adding, "Today's a new day, Jennifer and I just know that it will be a good one for you."

Jennifer knew that he was trying to put her in a good mood and appreciated the fact that he didn't pursue what happened at yesterday's meeting. Still, she just looked at him and said, "George, you don't want to know."

Sitting down at her desk was the last place she wanted to be. But as she settled in, taking her calendar and writing pad out of her briefcase, she noticed that a stack of return envelopes were sitting on the corner of her desk. Apparently, they had come in late yesterday after she had left. Jennifer quickly reached out to the envelopes, looking to first see if there were any "undeliverable" returns. To her surprise, she counted nine real responses. Maybe now, her luck was finally going to change.

While she was perusing the names and addresses of the prospects that sent in queries, she was interrupted by the overhead loudspeaker with Estelle's mellifluous voice, "all brokers please report to the conference room in five minutes for an urgent meeting."

Jennifer looked back at George, rolling her eyes. "Here we go again," she said. "Maybe it's another rabid POSOM."

George just smiled, not wanting to add more fuel to her fire. She joined him as he wheeled his chair into the conference room.

This time, Jennifer opted to sit in the back row. Lawrence grabbed the seat next to her. "Long time no see, pretty lady. What have you been up to?"

"Nothing much," Jennifer said. Clearly, she wasn't in the mood to discuss anything with this guy.

Still he persisted, "Really Jennifer, I haven't seen you, how's everything going with your prospecting?" Before she could just shut him up, he continued, "You know, I'm having my best month ever. My clients haven't done well with this lousy market, but I'm bringing in the gross. This could end up being my best year ever."

Jennifer couldn't have cared less. She thought that the word "gross," actually depicted him perfectly, he was just plain gross.

The conversation in the room stopped as soon as Lowell strode in. He had a smug look on his face. When he knew that he had the room's attention he started, "I have a surprise for you. Since we had a 100% participation in the last POSOM, I thought it only fair to reward you guys. As you know, Tate Yardley discourages their branch managers from actively producing. However, as it turns out, one of our top producers, Leonard Kahn decided to move on to another firm. Most of his clients followed him, but fortunately, I was able to snag one of his biggest clients. I went to visit her in Sarasota and we got along so well that I was able to sell her a few of our tax shelters. She ended up investing over $5 million dollars in three of our oil and gas deals. Needless to say, over $300,000 was generated in commissions. Since I can't keep it all, I'd like to award my branch with a portion of the gross. Depending on your annualized ranking in the office, each of you will receive a prorated amount. This will be reflective on your commission run at month's end. As you see, this proves my point, you help me in placing the POSOMS and other unattractive deals and I'll help you. One hand washes the other."

The room was jubilant. Clapping and cheering Lowell. Again, Jennifer was incredulous. She was thinking about how that poor woman had been taken such advantage of. From what she had read about the tax shelters, they were great for the firm and the brokers, paying a commission of 6% to 8%. But the customers were guaranteed of losing money. "O.K. everybody, let's get back to work," Lowell said.

The group trooped out of the conference room. Jennifer was walking alone back to the office when Lowell caught up with her. "Jennifer, since you're a new recruit, producing a marginal amount of business, you won't be included in this commission distribution. Once you really prove yourself to me, you'll be considered for future allocations." As he walked away from her he was thinking to himself that it would be a cold day in hell before he would help this broad.

When Jennifer got back to the office with George, he said, "You see what I mean about office politics? This is an ass-kissing business. You don't play the game right and you're excluded. It's truly unfortunate that the business has come to this. My best advice to you is to keep chiseling away. You will get a lucky break."

With this adversity, Jennifer became more motivated than ever. She looked through the names of respondents she had received and decided to focus in on a lady who listed her address in Palm Beach. She dialed the number, and a woman answered the phone with a Southern accent. "Good morning, this is Jennifer Palmer from Tate Yardley, are you Mrs. Cambridge?"

"Yes," the lady replied, "do I know you?"

"No," Jennifer said, "you mailed back a note to me asking that I phone you. Is this an inconvenient time?"

Mrs. Cambridge replied, "Oh, now I recall. It's just that I have a polo lesson in half an hour. Frankly, I'd rather meet you in person than speak on the phone. I really need help with my finances. How about meeting me for lunch at the 'Bath and Tennis,' the day after tomorrow? Do you know where that is?"

Jennifer's first reaction was one of hesitancy, especially after her prior experience. But the lady did sound nice and they were meeting in a neutral location. How bad could it be? "Mrs. Cambridge, I know just where the club is. What would be a convenient time for you?"

"Let's make it 1:00 p.m. I'll meet you at the reception. See you then."

After hanging up, Jennifer felt a tinge of excitement. At least it seemed that she would be meeting a nice lady, and she was quite familiar with the "Bath and Tennis." During high school her parents were members because the club had a magnificent tennis pro that had radically improved Jennifer's game.

After scoring great results with Mrs. Cambridge, Jennifer had a sense of cautious optimism. She was pumped up to forge ahead and phone the other respondents. A couple of the people she spoke with showed a high level of interest but indicated that they would get back to her. She left a voicemail message with three others who were not home and happily she was able to set up appointments in the office with a youngish sounding girl seeking guidance on how to start investing for her future. There were also two older couples who coincidentally lived at the same adult community. Jennifer staggered the appointments over the next ten days, making sure that she could secure the conference room. For the first time, she felt the satisfaction of really being on a roll.

Chapter 13

Jennifer spent the next day accumulating the necessary paperwork to take up to Palm Beach. If in fact, Mrs. Cambridge decided to move her account, she would need to sign Account Transfer (ACAT) papers to authorize the electronic transfer of the assets from firm to firm. Since Jennifer didn't enjoy the luxury of having a sales assistant, she had to hustle and secure the paperwork herself. Over the past several weeks, she had fortunately befriended George's assistant, Doris, who helped her put together the necessary paperwork. Doris was a forty-something lady, a little on the plump side, who had been working with George for over 15 years. She had a nice personality, similar to George and really felt empathy for Jennifer. She could appreciate the pressure Jennifer was experiencing as a recruit. Especially, working under a bastard like Lowell. She tried to go out of her way to assist Jennifer. There was so much compliance and regulation in the securities industry, that every "I" had to be dotted and every "t" had to be crossed.

One of the mutual fund wholesalers who frequently come to the branch to promote his funds had invited any interested brokers to lunch. The wholesaler typically would entertain at the best restaurant in town in hopes of getting more business from the brokers. Since Jennifer was spending the day preparing for her meeting the next day, she thought that it might be a good idea to attend the luncheon. If for nothing else, to get to know the other brokers in the office and hear what they were pitching to their clientele.

As the group was walking out to lunch, Jennifer nonchalantly joined them. Of course, Lawrence was there. Jennifer thought that he must not miss a meal. The others in the group took to her as a novelty. They were heading to Morton's, which was only two blocks from the office.

When they sat down, Lawrence immediately grabbed the seat next to Jennifer. "Someone has to take care of you," he said. Jennifer thought that was the last thing she needed. On her other side sat a broker who smiled at her and introduced himself as Howard. He was fairly slim with dark brown hair parted to the side. While they were looking over the menu, Howard asked Jennifer how she was enjoying her time so far at Tate Yardley.

Jennifer said, "It's been a challenge, probably the greatest in my life, but I'm just beginning to see some lights. How long have you been with the firm?" she asked.

"Ten long years. I wish I could retire but I have two twin girls about to enter college. Tuition is high and they are depending on me to generate enough in commissions to pay their way. With the tough market we've been experiencing, I've been trading my clients' accounts haphazardly just to earn a decent living. So far, no one has complained. Happily, it appears as though most of them don't even look at their statements, so I guess that's how I've gotten away with it so long." He then whispered to her, "But as bad as I am with trading, no one beats "Churn and Burn" Lawrence. He is the king of it in the office. He takes a vacation almost every six months, has half the assets of the average broker in the office and does twice the business."

Lawrence heard his name and smiling, said, "You two must be up to no good."

Howard nudged Jennifer with his arm and again whispered, "By the time Lawrence is done with them, they don't know what hit them." Jennifer was thinking that the insight Howard was giving her about the business certainly didn't jive with what she had experienced when she was younger with her father's broker. Maybe, she thought that this behavior was just isolated to a few greedy individuals. Surely, the entire industry couldn't practice in such a way. Or could it?

The waiter came by and the brokers ordered the most expensive items on the menu and the wholesaler didn't bat an eye. Apparently this was de rigueur in the business. If you attend these luncheons, you are expected to produce the business.

While they waited for the food, the wholesaler went into a brief explanation about his products and about what the portfolio managers in his company thought of the current market environment. Jennifer did garner a bit of insight, however, after the meal was served, the discussion turned to football and office gossip. Jennifer found that these guys were actually worse than women, on top of being totally immature as well as lacking any table manners.

When Jennifer got back to the office, she decided to review Tate Yardley's research in preparation of meeting her new client tomorrow. She chalked up her luncheon experience as one she would avoid in the future.

Chapter 14

Wednesday couldn't come soon enough for Jennifer. She woke up full of pep and vigor. The previous evening she had laid out her clothes, having decided to dress in a professional yet chic manner. Instead of a suit, she had selected a vibrant yellow classic Oscar de la Renta dress. It had sheer long sleeves with a soft ruffle around the neckline. She accessorized the dress simply with pearl Chanel earrings and beige Blahnik sling backs.

Jennifer got up early enough to fit in a four mile run. The exercise was not only great for her physically but when the endorphins kicked in, her mental acuity maxed out. Today, she wanted to be at the top of her game.

She stopped by the office to check in and make sure that her phone was covered. She also wanted to get a pulse of the market opening and the news of the day. At 11:00 Jennifer headed up to Palm Beach to meet Mrs. Cambridge. Even though it was a weekday, traffic was light so she actually arrived at the "Bath and Tennis" fifteen minutes early. She debated whether to drive around the island to kill time or to just valet the car and wait for Mrs. Cambridge. She opted for the latter since she didn't want to take any chances with local traffic. After all, it was still the height of the season. The front of the club was packed with rows of Bentleys, Rolls Royce's and Mercedes hugging the driveway. A few were occupied by chauffeurs patiently waiting for their employers to return. Jennifer proudly pulled up to the entrance in her red BMW. A uniformed valet immediately opened her door, saying, "Welcome to the Palm Beach Bath and Tennis Club, miss."

She grabbed her briefcase and bounded up the short flight of steps where another uniformed young man opened the door for her, again welcoming her to the club. She walked down a short marbled corridor to the reception desk. A pleasant looking woman in a tan dress greeted her. Jennifer said, "Hi, I'm Jennifer Palmer. I have a luncheon appointment with Mrs. Cambridge."

The receptionist smiled and said, "I see that Mrs. Cambridge left your name. You are the first to have arrived. Would you like to be seated in the dining room or would you prefer to wait here for Mrs. Cambridge?" Jennifer felt that it was only proper to wait and communicated that to the receptionist. "Please feel free to have a seat and make yourself comfortable. By the way, you won't be waiting long; Mrs. Cambridge is always on time." Jennifer took a seat on a white wicker sofa with plush bright pink and green flowered cushions. Beside the sofa was a table with a magazine, "Palm Beach Today." Jennifer picked it up perusing through the pages when the photo of an attractive red headed woman caught her eye. It was a full page spread. The title in big bold letters read, "Palm Beach's Woman of the Year: Mercedes Cambridge." Jennifer wondered if this possibly was the lady she was waiting to meet? She quickly read the article about how this Mrs. Cambridge was one of the most philanthropic members of the community. And about how she had provided college educations for dozens of underprivileged young people. The article went on to say that Mrs. Cambridge was a widow. Her husband had been the founder and chairman of one of the country's biggest steel companies. They had been married for over twenty years when he had unexpectedly died during a medical procedure. The article went on to explain that since the Cambridge's never had children of their own they were devoted to helping youngsters who didn't have the opportunity for an education. Since her husband's death, Mrs. Cambridge was dedicated to carrying on his spirit.

As she read that last sentence, Jennifer was startled by a well-dressed woman who had approached her extending her hand and with a slight Spanish accent said, "Hi, you must be Jennifer, I'm Mercedes Cambridge." As surprised as she was, Jennifer gracefully stood up and said, "Mrs. Cambridge, I'm so pleased to finally meet you." The lady was absolutely the woman profiled in the article Jennifer had just read. Wow, she thought, how fortunate she was to have read that article. At least she had a little insight into her luncheon companion.

Mrs. Cambridge said, "Jennifer, let's go into the dining room so we can talk." Jennifer let her lead the way. As they walked through, several of the diners stopped Mrs. Cambridge to chat. She was obviously a well known figure in Palm Beach society. When they made it to their table, Mrs. Cambridge took the seat looking out to the entrance of the dining room and motioned for Jennifer to take the seat to her right. Just as they were getting settled in, the maître'd came by to give Mrs. Cambridge a warm welcome. When the waiter walked over with menus, Mrs. Cambridge said, "Please give us a few minutes before taking our order, but bring us a bottle of Pellegrino with sliced lemons on the side." Pausing she looked at Jennifer and asked, "Jennifer, do you need to get back to your office soon, I don't want to linger if you have any time constraints?"

"No, Mrs. Cambridge, my time is yours."

Mrs. Cambridge looked sweetly at Jennifer and said, "Please darling, call me Mercedes." She then took out a folder containing her recent brokerage account statements. "Jennifer, I responded to your solicitation because I am just fed up. My husband, William, passed away last year and he always took care of our investments. Honestly, I barely had a clue as to what we owned. He managed everything. He was a very smart man. He founded one of the largest steel companies in the United States, but you would never know it. He was one of the most humble and considerate men on this planet. We had a wonderful love affair and I miss him terribly. I don't mean to ramble on, but I truly loved and respected him. We had the same stockbroker for the past ten or so years and it seemed as though William really trusted this man. They golfed together regularly at the club and had many friends in common. I always perceived him to be a bit of a social climber. After all, he doesn't live on 'the island,' and it seemed as though he took his last savings to join the club so he could meet the right people for his business. He and William seemed to have a convivial relationship. So, after his untimely death, I thought it best to leave our investments with this broker. Unfortunately, as it turns out, he hardly ever returns my calls, and when I do get him on the phone, he evades answering my questions and talks about the club and what a strong person I've become since my husband's death. He doesn't seem to understand that I don't need patronizing, just answers to my questions. I may not be an investment maven, but I did graduate summa cum laude from Smith with a degree in Fine Arts.

It doesn't take a rocket scientist to review a brokerage account statement and discern that things don't appear right. From the looks of things, it appears that he has been doing quite a bit of trading in the account, without my knowledge. Additionally, the value of the account looks to have decreased considerably over the last six months. I have had many a sleepless night over this and need an objective party to give me advice. Jennifer, why don't you take a look at my statement?"

Mercedes handed a folder containing her statement over to Jennifer. She glanced at the first page, which showed an account value of

$8.3 million dollars. Without reacting, she proceeded to the account activity. There were at least 30 trades that occurred for the month long period of time. At the end of the statement was the gain/loss page. Mercedes had lost over two million dollars year to date, which so far, was a period of four months. Jennifer noticed that all the assets were invested in equities. There were no bonds or any other type of fixed income. By looking at the statement, Mercedes' account was being traded irrationally. Jennifer knew that she had to be diplomatic and didn't want to alarm her.

"Mercedes, let me begin by saying that I'm sure your broker had your best interest at heart." Jennifer was practically choking on her words. She continued, "But obviously, all your assets are exposed to risk and there is no asset allocation or balance to your portfolio. From what you are telling me, you need exposure to fixed income, dividend paying stocks, even CDs. Maybe your late husband wanted a portfolio more exposed to risk, but with your current circumstances, I would recommend a more conservative approach."

Mercedes smiled at Jennifer and replied, "I knew that there was something about you I liked. Not only are you beautiful but smart. Jennifer, I want you to manage this account. You prove yourself to me and over time there will be more for you to manage. Now let's order lunch, shall we?"

Mercedes called the waiter over, and ordered a crabmeat stuffed avocado, recommending the same for Jennifer. "You will love this signature dish; the club makes the combination of lump meat crab and avocado with a light remoulade sauce simply delicious. I just know you will enjoy it."

The waiter brought over warm sourdough rolls and replenished their glasses. While the two ladies were engaging in conversation, a tall handsome young man came by the table to greet Mercedes. They were quite happy to see each other. He gave her a big hug and a kiss on the cheek. "Jennifer, this is Javier, he is the son of my dearest friends. Javier is in a similar business as yours, but he only handles accounts in the billions, forget millions. Javier, please meet my new broker Jennifer Palmer."

Javier took Jennifer's hand and gave it a light kiss. Jennifer immediately felt the electricity flow through her body. She thought he was quite good looking. He was dressed impeccably, with a blue blazer, white crisp open shirt, gold cuff links and tan gabardine slacks. He had dark hair, combed back off his face and captivating brown eyes. With his darker complexion, his smile lit up the room. "Jennifer Palmer," he said with a slight Spanish accent, "it is indeed a true pleasure to meet you."

Wow, Jennifer thought, she hadn't felt her heart race like this in a long time. Since her dis-engagement from Brook, she had thrown herself into her career Even though she was working in a male dominated world; she had no interest in her male counterparts. From Lowell on down, she viewed her colleagues as glorified salesmen. Plus, she had set her mind on not getting involved in a relationship. Dating was not a high priority in her life. That was until now. She could feel herself flushing when Javier took her hand. As he spoke with Mercedes, Jennifer subtly glanced at his ring finger. It was unadorned. But she thought, a gorgeous guy like this must have girlfriends. He asked her if she lived in Palm Beach. She told him that she was currently living in Coconut Grove, "But I drive up to Palm Beach quite often." After she said it, she felt like an idiot for making such stupid comment.

He said, "Well, I drive down to Coral Gables at least twice a month. One of our clients has his corporate headquarters in the Gables." The more Javier spoke, the more Jennifer could feel the warmth rising up her body. After he and Mercedes finished their conversation, he extended his hand again to Jennifer saying, "I look forward to sharing your company again."

Mercedes immediately stepped in. "Javier, I'll make sure of it."

He leaned down and gave Mercedes a kiss on both cheeks, adding, "I'm so glad to have seen you today." With that, he strode out of the dining room. Jennifer sneaked a glance at his tight little tush.

Mercedes looked at Jennifer. "You lit up like a Christmas tree. I don't want to be presumptuous, but are you married or involved with anyone?" Mercedes asked.

"Frankly, Mercedes, I have been so focused on my career, that I haven't even gone out on a date in the last six months."

"Such a pity, a beautiful young lady like yourself, being deprived for the sake of business. That's utterly ridiculous. What did you think of think of tall, dark and handsome Javier? Before you answer, he's not your typical Latin lover. I've known his parents forever. They're Colombian. His father was the head of Exxon, South America. They always kept a home here on the island for holidays. Javier has never been married because he just never found the right girl. His parents brought him up the old-fashioned way. He's a real gentleman just like his father. He graduated with an MBA from Wharton, interned at a hedge fund on Wall Street and decided after learning the ropes to form his own fund. His accounts are mainly institutional. I guess they have to be, because his minimum investment requirement is $5 million. Apparently he's done quite well for himself as well as for his clients. He recently built a home next door to his parents' house here on the island. He's an accomplished polo player and is quite social. We always seem to run into each other at the different charity functions. Before I go on with my idea, it seemed as though there was a mutual attraction between the two of you. Now, tell me what you think."

Jennifer was overwhelmed. First she had just possibly landed an account that could really launch her career and then on top of that, she met a guy who was just impossibly irresistible. "Mercedes, I'm ready, tell me your idea."

"Jennifer, the Red Cross Ball is coming up next month and I bought two tables. I would just adore inviting you and Javier to join me. We would have a great time. The event is exactly three weeks from this Saturday. Would you be available?"

Before she even completed the last syllable of "available," Jennifer said, "What should I wear?"

Mercedes smiled. "It's black-tie and I'm sure whatever you select will be perfect. Jennifer, you're my kind of girl. You and I are going to have a lot of fun together. And the best part is that you're going to protect my money at the same time." The waiter was just placing their luncheon platters on the table. Mercedes raised her glass of Pellegrino and said, "Jennifer, I look forward to a long friendship with you." They clinked their glasses and began to eat. Jennifer took special notice of the presentation of her dish. The china was her favorite Villeroy and Bosch Country French. The food looked delectable. The avocado was a perfect almost chartreuse color stuffed with the pink lump meat crab. The plate was garnished with watercress and a sliced hardboiled egg. The remoulade sauce was served on the side. Mercedes was right, the food was exceptional. During the meal, Jennifer asked Mercedes how she had met her husband. She told her that they had met while she was attending Smith College. "William was at Harvard finishing up his senior year and I was a junior at Smith. We met at a 'Howdy Doody Dance,' and honestly Jennifer, it was love at first sight. He was a terrific dancer and he literally swept me off my feet. Within six months, he took me home to meet his parents and mine flew in to Boston to meet him. Everyone got along. But most importantly, we did. He proposed to me on his graduation day, right in front of John Harvard's statue on campus. I was so ecstatically speechless, that he didn't wait for my answer, but placed the engagement ring right on my finger. You see, I still haven't taken it off."

Jennifer noticed tears welling up in Mercedes' eyes. She reached out to her with comforting words, "Mercedes, you are so lucky to have experienced love in your life. Do you know how many people have gone through their lives and have never been in love? You have to be so grateful for having had a true love of your life."

Mercedes took a sip of the water and collected her emotions. "My dear, you are so right and now we are going to focus on a new love in your life. How does that sound?" Mercedes smiled and drew Jennifer to her, giving her a kiss on the head. "You've spent way too much time with me. You need to get back to your office. Let me walk you out to the valet."

As they walked out of the dining room together, Mercedes slipped her arm through Jennifer's and said, "I'm so glad you sent me that note of solicitation otherwise we would have never met. I feel so comfortable with you and am pleased to have you as my new broker. When should I expect your receipt of my account?"

"Mercedes, typically the transfer can take up to ten business days, but I will let you know as soon as I receive notification from the opposing firm. I too am so pleased to have had the privilege of meeting you. I will not disappoint you. Thank you so much for lunch."

Jennifer's car was waiting at the porte coucheur. Mercedes gave her a quick kiss on the cheek and wished her a safe drive back. Just as Jennifer was getting in her car, she heard Mercedes call out, "Don't be surprised if you get a call from Javier. Speak with you soon."

On the drive back to the office, Jennifer couldn't believe her good fortune of meeting Mercedes. Bringing in an $8 million account would definitely keep Lowell off her back and secure her position at Tate Yardley. Beside the business aspect, she had met a lovely lady and was looking forward to a long and mutually rewarding relationship. Not to mention the debonair Javier. Jennifer wondered if and when she would hear from him.

Chapter 15

For the first time, Jennifer entered the offices of Tate Yardley with a secure and almost carefree attitude. She had decided not to tell anyone about her meeting with Mercedes. They'll find out soon enough when the account is received.

When Jennifer entered the office she shared with George, he immediately detected her happier spirit. Not wanting to pry, he looked up from the computer monitor and said, "Welcome back, Jennifer, I trust you had a better day than I have. The market is getting killed today. It was down over 500 points earlier and has now retraced about 200 points."

"George, what in the hell happened to cause such a decline?"

"There is a rumor out there, probably initiated by the shorts that a large French bank is on the brink of insolvency. The bank has been making statements all day, denying the rumor. The ECB just came out saying that they have the wherewithal to back any bank collapse. It's just crazy. Enough of that, you look happy, how did your meeting go?"

"It was very interesting and appears to be quite promising. I'd prefer not to discuss it. Just don't want to jinx it. Any new gossip around here?"

"Just the same old stuff, Lowell came around earlier, asking where you were. I told him that you had a client meeting. He started asking questions and I just told him to give you a little breathing room. If it's difficult for an old broker-veteran like me to attract assets in these tumultuous times, I can just imagine what you're going through."

Jennifer was annoyed that Lowell was on her case, but hopefully she thought, the new account coming in should shut him up. "Oh, by the way," George said, "there's a mandatory meeting in the big conference room at 8:30 a.m. tomorrow. There's probably a new product they want us to sell that's guaranteed to make the firm money."

Just as George finished his sentence, Lowell popped his head in the office. "Hi guys, its 3:30, you've got half an hour more to generate commissions." As he walked away, Jennifer looked at George and rolled her eyes.

As George's phone began to ring, she turned back to her desk and reviewed her calendar. First, she marked the Saturday for the Red Cross Ball that Mercedes had invited her to. She had always read about how that was one of the most beautiful balls of the season. No matter what, she had to make the time to go shopping for an elegant gown. Maybe this weekend she would go up to the Bal Harbor shops and start the search. Between Saks and Neiman's she was bound to find something unique. She noticed that she had an 11:00 a.m. meeting the next day with one of the older couples she had spoken with earlier in the week. They had sounded sweet on the phone and she was looking forward to meeting them. She looked at her computer and saw that it was almost 4:00 p.m. and the industrial average was closing down just over 300 points. The only good thing about being a new broker was that she didn't have any concerns about clients' portfolios. But seeing how treacherous the financial markets are of late, she would take extra precautions not to over-expose her new clients to undue risk. She was determined not to let the firm's propaganda or Lowell's tactics influence her in any way. Happily, she wasn't married with children to support or for that matter, herself to support. Even though her parents weren't thrilled about her chosen profession, they had stuck by her, providing anything and everything she could possibly need. Once the new assets start coming in, Jennifer was committed to moving out and supporting herself.

Chapter 16

The next morning, Jennifer was seated in the conference room, observing the group of fellow brokers meandering in. Up to now, she had only spoken with a few of them. She sensed that many of them viewed her as a competitive threat. Every day now, Lowell distributed a list of the brokers' commission production. It reflected a list of who had done what the prior day as well as a list of who was ahead for the month and the year to date. It seemed as though they were all vying to have their name occupy the top tier of the list. Jennifer couldn't believe the emphasis placed on the list. The markets had been so volatile as of late, so she couldn't imagine what kind of business the top brokers were doing. She assumed that they were either like Lawrence, who really didn't seem to care and just was looking to make money for himself or they were serious brokers, who over time had accumulated a vast amount of assets through unique contacts or just plain luck, and despite market conditions, they always had money to place. She had heard that the top broker in the office, James Caldwell III, had assets of over a billion dollars. Rumor had it, that most of the money he had under management was old family money. He had inherited his book from his father, JC III (a case of luck), who had also been a top broker at the firm before retiring. James knew that his production (well over $3 million a year), carried a large percentage of the office and used his clout to get just about anything he wanted, including first right of refusal on any hot new IPOs and unlimited expense account. He drove a red Ferrari and never went out of his way to speak with his colleagues. Jennifer figured that he really didn't have to. The consistently ranked number two broker in the office, Manuel Luis Cordova, was from Colombia. He managed over $500 million, generating about $1.5 million in commissions. Most of his clients were Colombians. Apparently, there was a steady flow of funds emanating from Latin America. And much of it seemed to find a home with Manuel. As opposed to JC III, Manuel was a very cordial man, always with a smile on his face. Jennifer recalled that he was one of the first brokers who had come by her desk to welcome her to the firm.

In sharp contrast to the "top producers" of the office, Jennifer could sense pretty readily the lower tier. It was if there was an unspoken caste system. Those brokers who generated lower overall commissions were treated almost like lepers. To start with, Jennifer noticed that their names were always relegated to the bottom of the daily production list. So right away, they were singled out. They were required to attend all firm functions, no matter how inconvenient as well as brown nose Lowell for fear of being let go. Worst of all, they had to spend two evenings a week in the office cold-calling lists of unsuspecting prospects. After seeing how they were mistreated, Jennifer was determined not to be included in their ranks. As the brokers continued to file into the conference room, she noticed how the low producers had to sit in the first few rows. The sad fact was, Jennifer thought, that some of these "low producers," might be actually putting their clients' interests ahead of their own. Perhaps they were looking to do right by their clients instead of making the fast bucks. No matter what, Jennifer just knew in her soul that she would be successful, but still would always be ethical in her dealings. With that thought in mind, Lowell strode in. This time he was accompanied by two men that Jennifer had never met before. As he walked to the front of the conference room, he was patting backs and making small talk with a few of the "big producers." He began by saying to the group, "Well guys, we just started the fourth quarter of the year and I'm sure you recall what our goal is for the year: $25 million. We have less than three months now to get there. I'm well aware of the fact that we have been encountering a treacherous market environment. But despite that, if you each generate eight thousand more a month in gross we'll achieve our goal. And as I previously mentioned, you do that for me and I will make sure we have an over the top celebration. Now, our regional director, Don Maroone would like to say a few words."

A tall, slim middle-aged man approached the podium. He had short, brown wavy hair and piercing blue eyes, wearing rimless glasses, which gave him a severe look. He was wearing a gray suit with a yellow tie. Though slim, Jennifer noticed that he had quite a rotund mid-drift. As he began to speak, she was surprised that he never unbuttoned his jacket. It looked as though his jacket would pop. Jennifer had vaguely recalled that he was the "boss of bosses." Apparently, Lowell and all the branch managers reported to Maroone, as well as all the complex managers. He was responsible for the Southeastern region from Tallahassee all the way down to Puerto Rico. Supposedly, his appearance in a branch would evoke terror. He made the ultimate decision of hiring and firing. He also commanded the opening and closings of the branches. He was a no-nonsense manager, who ruled by the numbers. Jennifer heard that he was so tough that the joke was that he had acid instead of blood running through his veins. The brokers were quite curious as to his visit at the Miami office.

"Ladies and gentlemen, I'm sure you're all wondering why I'm here today. It's quite simple. Your branch has consistently been in the top 5% of the country and I want to make sure you maintain your position.

Lowell has done a great job as branch manager and I'm sure you don't want to disappoint him. I'm personally here today to appeal to each and every one of you to set your sights on accomplishing the branch year end goal. Even though we are going through a challenging time in the world markets, Tate Yardley has the products that can appeal to any of your clients. And by the way, if there is something we don't have, and you have the clients with dollars to invest, we can create a customized product just for your client base. Remember guys, we're closing in on the year-end quickly, and it's up to each of you to contribute your fair share. I'm confident that you will do whatever it takes to assist Lowell in achieving his goal. Now for our last speaker today, we've brought down John Chastain from New York to discuss products in his area that if presented the right way, can be sold to any of your clients. John, the floor is yours."

"Oh, John, just give me one more quick minute. You know guys, you're lucky to be working at the biggest and most highly regarded brokerage firm in the world. I have lists of brokers at other firms that are just waiting for you to screw up, so they'll have their turn at bat here. I just know you won't disappoint me. Now John, the floor is yours."

While John embarked on his sales spiel, Jennifer was once again incredulous with what she had just heard. Basically, Lowell and the "Boss of Bosses," were telling them to do whatever it takes to generate commissions to achieve their year-end agenda. Once again, the tone of the presentation was a hard sell appeal to line the pockets of the firm with absolutely no regard to the clients. Jennifer couldn't help thinking that maybe her parents had been right about this profession, if you could call it that. Surely, she thought, there must be ethical brokers that don't fall for this kind of "dog and pony" show and are motivated to protect their clients' money. She knew for a fact that George, her office mate, was a broker with integrity. But she couldn't help thinking about "Churn and Burn" Lawrence and Howard, the broker with kids in college, who sat next to her at the wholesaler luncheon. He literally told her that he was doing whatever he could get away with to earn a living. And these were just two brokers she knew about. John Chastain continued on with his Power Point presentation, espousing the advantages of each of the products he discussed. When he finally concluded, Lowell took to the podium once again. "Thank you all for coming this morning. In advance, thank you all for your hard work and I look forward to our celebratory dinner. Make it great day!"

Jennifer was walking back to her office, when her "old friend" Lawrence caught up to her. "Hey Jen, how's it going?" Before she could even reply, he continued on, "even though it's only October, I've already achieved my year-end goal. I think I'll check out a Christmas cruise on the Internet. How about lunch today? You know, a guy can take only so many turndowns."

Annoyed with Lawrence and his thieving ways, Jennifer still managed to give him her innocent little smile and said, "Lawrence, I'm so pleased for you and your achievements. Remember, I'm just the rookie here, just trying to aspire to your success. I need to work. No lunches for a while. But thanks for thinking of me." She thought how much he irritated her with his smug attitude.

When Jennifer got back to her office, she noticed a pink message slip taped to her phone. She picked it up and saw that Javier Cordova had called. He left his office and cell numbers with a message for Jennifer to return his call at her convenience. Her heart was pounding and she could feel the flush on her face. She noticed that he had called about 20 minutes earlier. Maybe it would be better if she waited a little longer to call him back. After all, she didn't want to appear too anxious, even though she could barely contain her excitement. Mercedes was right, but Jennifer didn't think she would hear from him so soon.

She went ahead preparing for the day's activities, logging on to her computer and checking the e-mails to see the morning's reports from equity and fixed income research. Included in her e-mails was one from an unfamiliar address: pbmercedes@aol.com. Jennifer cautiously opened it and in moments was pleasantly surprised to see it was from her new client, Mercedes Cambridge. It read, "Jennifer, I really enjoyed meeting you yesterday, can't wait to get started on my account. By the way, you should be hearing from Javier today. He called me yesterday evening for your contact information. He's a good one. Don't let him get away." She signed it, "Best, MC." A P.S. was added to the bottom of the message, "Mailed you the invitation to the Red Cross Ball."

Jennifer liked the way Mercedes followed up with her. Actually, she felt that it was really her responsibility to have written to Mercedes first, but at the end of the day, it probably didn't matter. Still, she responded to the message, "Mercedes, it was my pleasure to meet you. I look forward to assisting you achieve your financial goals. I will notify you once your account arrives at Tate Yardley safe and sound. Can't wait to receive the Red Cross invitation and by the way, heard from Javier earlier today. Kindest Regards, Jennifer."

While Jennifer was on her computer, she decided to Google Mercedes. Surprisingly nothing came up except the fact that she was a resident of Palm Beach County. She then tried Googling the magazine, *Palm Beach Today,* where she had read the article about Mercedes. Again nothing came up. Jennifer pulled up the archive section of the site, to pull up specific articles in the past about Mercedes Cambridge. Not a mention appeared. Jennifer assumed that the article was probably too recent to appear on the website yet. She concluded that Mercedes had probably blocked anything about her appearing on Google for security reasons. A widow with such vast wealth has to be careful about having her name appear on the Internet.

Since she was in the Googling mood, she put Javier's name in the search engine. When she hit the enter button, at least three pages came up about Javier. She opened the window titled, "Javier Cordova, up and coming hedge fund manager." She learned that he was in fact single (a good sign), with a tremendous investment track record. The article said that he had been racking up double digit returns for his clients for the last several years. It noted that even in the worst investment climate in years, Javier had maintained profitable results for his clients. He was called the new up and coming money manager with the "Midas touch." She saw that there was an excerpt from *Forbes* magazine, describing Javier as one of the leading hedge fund managers of the decade. Apparently, as she read on, he had made a huge bet shorting the S & P index. The position resulted in huge profits, totaling several billion dollars for his clients, which as a hedge fund manager, he also participated in.

Jennifer was duly impressed. She had read enough, Javier definitely played in the big leagues and she was looking forward to meeting him again. She looked at her watch and saw that it had been over an hour since he had called.

She picked up the phone and dialed his number. A woman answered the phone, "Cordova Investments."

Jennifer said, "I'd like to speak with Javier Cordova."

The receptionist responded, "Who may I ask is calling?"

"It's Jennifer Palmer, returning Mr. Cordova's call."

"Let me see if he's available."

Jennifer was placed on hold for mere seconds before she heard Javier's mellifluous voice. "Jennifer, it is so nice to hear from you. I will be in Miami today and would like to invite you to have lunch with me. I know it's a bit last minute, so I would surely understand if you couldn't join me."

Jennifer thought quickly. First she looked down at herself to see what she was wearing; a Von Furstenberg yellow wrap dress and black peephole stilettos. The wardrobe passed her critical inspection. Now, would she appear too available to accept a luncheon invitation at the last minute? She reasoned to herself that it was lunch not dinner, so why not?

"Javier, as it turns out, I can make it."

"That's just what I was hoping to hear. Tell me where you are located and I will come by and pick you up around one o'clock."

Jennifer gave him the office address and they agreed that he would phone her from his car when he was downstairs. He wanted to park and come up to the office but she felt that it would be better to meet him downstairs. After they hung up, Jennifer felt a flutter run through her body. She was pleased that this guy didn't waste any time.

Taking a look at the monitor, she saw that the markets were once again opening down. Jennifer had been so distracted with Javier that she'd nearly forgotten that she had an 11:30 meeting scheduled with the older couple who had responded to her previous solicitation. She was meeting Javier around 1:00, so an hour and a half should give her plenty of time with the new prospects. She quickly hustled to retrieve all the documentation necessary to open a new account, as well as some of the firm's research reports to use for recommendations.

Before she knew it, the receptionist called and informed her that the couple had arrived and were waiting in the lobby. Jennifer grabbed her paperwork, dropped it off in the conference room and went out to meet her new clients. They looked to be in their mid-seventies and seemed friendly. Jennifer guided them to the conference room where they all took their seats. Jennifer let them start by telling her their financial concerns and objectives. She responded by elaborating on her background and how she could help them. They seemed pleased with her presentation and wanted to move forward with opening an account. They had $300,000 to invest and wanted to derive as much income from the initial investment without touching the principal. Together they completed and signed all of the suitability paperwork. They agreed with Jennifer to focus primarily on fixed income and that she would call them before any transactions were executed. Jennifer was happy to open a new account and was looking forward to helping the couple achieve their financial goals. As she walked them out, she stole a quick glance at her watch. It was 12:45, and hopefully Javier hadn't called yet. After bidding her new clients goodbye, Jennifer made a mad dash back to her office. She was relieved not to see any messages.

At precisely 1:00, her phone rang. As she answered it she heard, "Jennifer, it's me. I'm parked right outside the front doors."

Jennifer was surprised that Javier was right on time. "I'm on my way," she said cheerfully. With that, she grabbed her handbag and headed out the door, stopping at the receptionist to let her know that she would be out and to take messages.

Chapter 17

As Jennifer walked out the front doors, she saw a red Ferrari parked in the circular driveway awaiting her arrival with Javier behind the wheel. He immediately jumped out of the car and greeted her with a kiss on her cheek and opened the passenger door. He seemed to be genuinely happy to see Jennifer. While settling into the driver's seat he said, "Jennifer, you look even more beautiful than I remember, and I am so happy you could meet me for lunch. Instead of driving to Coral Gables, I thought we might dine right around the corner at the Four Seasons. Is that all right with you?"

Jennifer looked over at this gorgeous man with big brown eyes. "Javier, the Four Seasons will be perfect." While he started the car and raced down the driveway, she took her own personal inventory of her luncheon date. His brown hair was brushed back with just the right amount of wave that let it fall slightly over his forehead. He was wearing a starched black and white striped shirt with the letters JLC embroidered on the cuffs, and a pair of black slacks with a black alligator Hermes belt. She looked down, and saw that he was wearing black suede Tod's. Behind the driver's seat was an ivory jacket. She never understood why so many men wore their jackets when they were driving. Javier had certainly passed Jennifer's wardrobe test with flying colors.

Not only was Javier "easy on the eyes," but his scent was absolutely intoxicating. As he was driving, he said, "So Jennifer, how has your morning been? I hope well."

Jennifer said, "I had to attend a sales meeting this morning and it was so hard sell. All they seem to care about at my firm is bringing in the commissions. It's truly pathetic."

"My dear, that's how the big firms make money. I started my career interning at a hedge fund while I was attending Wharton. I never wanted to work for a big Wall Street firm precisely for the reason you have just stated. At least at the hedge funds, the company doesn't really make the big bucks until their clients have. At a firm like yours, the company makes a fortune while the clients win or lose. In fact, at my firm, with the recent volatile market conditions, we just lowered our standard client fees. We want our clients to make money. We are not in the business of nickel and diming."

They approached the entranceway to the Four Seasons and two valets ran over to them. While one helped Jennifer out, she heard the other valet saying, "Welcome, Mr. Cordova, it's so nice to see you again. We'll keep your car parked up here in the driveway." He helped Javier on with his jacket. "Is there anything else we can do for you?"

Jennifer knew that the Four Seasons hotels were known for their personalized service, but to greet Javier by name was over the top. She guessed that he was a regular guest at the hotel. As they walked into the lobby together she could feel his arm lightly touch her waist, and immediately experienced the same spark of electricity as when he kissed her hand in Palm Beach. They headed toward the restaurant, which had a beautiful view of the bay. The maître'd welcomed them in. "Mr. Cordova, it's so nice to see you again. Would you prefer your regular table outside?"

"Jay that would be fine. It's such a beautiful day." They were led to a table set for four right near the water's edge. There was a glass balcony rail next to the table so the view was unobstructed. On the same level of the restaurant, Jennifer could see an infinity pool surrounded by modern wicker furniture. She noticed quite a few guests swimming in the pool and sunbathing. The maitre'd took away the extra place settings and presented them with menus. While Jennifer opened her menu, she noticed that Javier just put his aside. A waiter came over, introducing himself and asking them for their beverage selection. Jennifer ordered a Perrier and Javier requested that the waiter just bring over a liter bottle of Perrier which they would share.

As soon as the waiter departed, Javier touched Jennifer's arm and said, "I have to admit that since we met yesterday, I have not stopped thinking about you. I couldn't wait to get your number from Mercedes. And I must admit, I told you a little white lie. I did not have an appointment in Miami today; I just was determined to see you. If you had been unavailable for lunch, I would have tried inviting you for a coffee or plan B, inviting you for dinner. I was compelled to spend time with you today. Now Jennifer, please tell me about you."

Jennifer was pleasantly shocked at hearing his words. She would never admit to him that she too hadn't stopped thinking of him since yesterday. In fact, she had dreamt about him last night. As she started speaking to him about herself, he took her hand and the gaze of his big brown eyes never seemed to leave her face. The waiter, who had previously tried several times to take their order, approached their table again, timidly asking, "Have you both decided on anything?"

Jennifer had done so much talking that she still hadn't looked at the menu and frankly the butterflies in her stomach had quelled any appetite. To appease the waiter, Javier asked, "What are your specials today? Wait, do you still have the Caesar salad with rock shrimp?"

"Indeed we do sir. Is that what you would like to have?"

Javier looked over at Jennifer. "It's a fantastic salad, they make the dressing eggless, and so it's light and delicious. If you like a good Caesar salad, I know you will enjoy it."

Clearly smitten just with being in Javier's company, Jennifer nodded her head. The waiter happily headed off to finally place their order. Javier then said, "I am so intrigued by what you have told me about yourself. Not only are you beautiful but you are smart and cultured. I have been searching for someone like you. Now let me tell you a little about myself." Javier proceeded to tell Jennifer about how he was raised in Bogota, Colombia, and how his parents sent him to the States for his education. He had attended Exeter and then went on to Wharton for his undergraduate and MBA degree. He had a large family, two sisters and two brothers. The family had always maintained a home in Palm Beach. He also spoke three languages and his family had afforded him the luxury of traveling all over the world. He told her a little about his hedge fund and about the type of clients he deals with.

While he was speaking, Jennifer was thinking about how physically attracted she was to him. She even thought about how he would make love to her. At the same time, she recalled what she had read on Google about him. She just loved being with an accomplished man. As he finished giving Jennifer a snapshot of his background, he said, "In all my travels and all my experiences, my most memorable place to be is sitting next to Jennifer Palmer, right here and right now."

Needless to say, Jennifer was floored by that comment. He then took her hand and gave it a kiss. The waiter reappeared with their salads and they kept talking, barely touching their food. Jennifer could tell how excited Javier was. She felt so comfortable with him. They seemed to take turns ending sentences for each other. Despite their different backgrounds, she was surprised as to how much they had in common. When the waiter came back to clear their plates and ask if they wanted anything else, Jennifer took a glance at her watch. She couldn't believe it was just past 4:00. They had been sitting there for over three hours, oblivious of time. Unfortunately, Jennifer knew that she had to report back to work, but she just didn't want their luncheon to end. "Javier, I hate to tell you this, but I really must get back to work. I have adored the time we have spent together and I am so happy that you drove down to see me."

Javier replied, "Jennifer, I certainly had no intention of keeping you away from your office so long. Let me get the check and I'll take you right back. But first, you have to tell me when I can see you again. Are you free for this Saturday evening?"

Under normal circumstances, Jennifer would never accept a Saturday night date so late in the week, but she couldn't resist. "Javier Saturday sounds great."

"Jennifer, I have an idea. Why don't I send a car for you and we'll have dinner in Palm Beach. If you would like, I can arrange a room for you at the Brazilian Court and then we can spend the next day together and I'll drive you back home in the afternoon. How do you like that plan?"

"Javier, I look forward to it."

"Then I take that as a yes?"

"Yes," Jennifer said and reached out to squeeze his arm.

Javier paid the bill, got up and helped Jennifer out of her seat. They walked out of the restaurant holding hands. As promised, Javier's Ferrari was parked right out front of the hotel. While getting in the car, the valets offered each of them a bottle of water for the ride back. Within minutes, they had arrived in the front of Jennifer's building. Javier turned to her and said, "Jennifer, this has truly been a wonderful afternoon. I so look forward to seeing you on Saturday night. Make sure to pack sport clothes for Sunday, if the weather is nice we might go horseback riding on a couple of my polo ponies." He looked at her with his gorgeous eyes and drew her near to him, giving her a soft kiss on the lips. Javier immediately got out of the car to open her door. "I will phone you tomorrow and let you know when to expect my driver." He gave her a warm hug and bid her good-bye. Jennifer walked into the building toward the bank of elevators feeling the heat arising in her body.

Wow, she thought what an afternoon. She felt as though she were already falling in love with this man that she had only met 24 hours ago. Maybe, "love at first sight," still existed in the 21st century. She certainly hoped so.

Chapter 18

That night at dinner, Jennifer deliberated with herself about how she was going to tell her parents about Javier. She decided just to tell them the plain truth. After all, she was no longer a child, but she felt obligated to tell them about her weekend plans since she was still living under their roof. As they were being served the arroz con pollo that Melidia had made, Jennifer started the conversation. "You know, I was in Palm Beach yesterday and opened the largest account of my career thus far."

Her father interrupted her, "Jen, that's terrific! Is he a physician?"

"No Dad, she's a widow of a big industrialist and we got along charmingly well. In fact, while we were at the club, she introduced me to a young man whom she has known forever. His family has a house right next to hers. So today he came down to have lunch with me. We had a fabulous time and he invited me to have dinner with him in Palm Beach on Saturday night. He asked me to spend the night, reserving a room for me at a local hotel so we can go horseback riding the next day."

Her parents looked at each other disapprovingly.

"Look Dad and Mom, I'm not asking your permission to go, I just want to give you the courtesy of knowing my plans so you won't be worried about me. He's really a great guy. As I told you, my new client introduced me to him and I even Googled him today. He owns one of the highest rated hedge funds in the country. He's been written up in *Forbes* magazine. I can't wait for you both to meet him."

"Jennifer, we know it's not in our place anymore to tell you what to do. Plus, if we did, you're a strong-headed young lady and would do what you wanted to do. But, please be careful. In this day and age, anything is possible. Of course we're not thrilled with this idea, but just please leave us his name and number and the hotel you will be staying at. You are our only daughter, we just want the very best for you."

Great, Jennifer thought, at least that hurdle was over with. As soon as they finished dinner, she went up to her room to decide what she would pack for her weekend rendezvous.

When Jen finally made it to bed, she thought about how much she enjoyed her afternoon with Javier. Just thinking about him got her sexually excited. With his good looks, charm and intelligence, she thought that maybe she had finally met her match. It would really be a blessing if things worked out.

The next morning, Jennifer arrived at the office with an air of anticipation. She couldn't wait to hear from Javier. Even George noticed a change in her. "Boy, Jennifer, you seem very happy today. I had an appointment out of the office yesterday before you returned; did you open another new account?"

"No George, it's a guy I met. He's cute, sweet and smart. And best of all, he appears to be head over heels with me. I'm not going to use the word, love. But this may be the one, George."

"Jennifer, I'm happy for you, but take it from me, don't rush into anything. Time will tell you if he's the right one."

"Thanks, George, for your sage advice. I'll keep you posted." Just as she finished her sentence the phone rang, she looked at the Caller ID, and it displayed JC Investments. It was Javier. Her heart skipped a beat as she answered, "Jennifer Palmer, may I help you?"

"Jennifer darling, it's Javier. I've missed you so and thought about you all through the night. Darling Jennifer, I'm calling to let you know that my personal driver, Miguel, will pick you up tomorrow evening at 6:30. That should give us enough time for you to make it up here, have a cocktail and then enjoy dinner. I've secured a reservation Café Europe, if that's all right with you?"

"Javier, I'm sure wherever you select will be lovely. Let me give you my address and home phone number. I'm still temporarily living with my parents, and they would like to have your home phone number as well in case they need to get hold of me. And Javier, I can't wait to see you as well."

Jennifer normally wasn't so demonstrative at the beginning of a relationship, but felt that this was too important to play games with. She gave Javier directions and the address to her house, hanging up the phone with that now familiar warmth of desire creeping back through her body. Of course, she knew that she first had to get through one more day of the week before enjoying the fruits of the weekend.

Per usual, the markets slithered down for the opening bell. News from Europe regarding possible bank defaults did little to raise spirits. However, nothing could dampen Jennifer's spirits. She even received notification that Mercedes' account was in the process of being transferred to Tate Yardley. Jennifer knew that if she had received the notice, Lowell certainly had also been informed. She was curious to see if he would come by and congratulate her as she often saw him do with the others, or simply ignore it. She certainly wasn't going to broach the news to him. Jennifer proceeded to call Mercedes and inform her that her account was en route to the firm. She called her right after

10:00 a.m. and after one ring Mercedes answered the phone with an upbeat tone to her voice. Jennifer let her know about the notice she had received and told her that the account should be settled at Tate Yardley by Tuesday morning.

Mercedes sounded so happy to hear from her. "Jennifer, you're a woman of your word. Now, if you can just start turning my account around, I'll be forever grateful. How are things going with you?"

Jennifer debated telling Mercedes about meeting with Javier, but figured she would find out from him so why not? "Mercedes, I had lunch with Javier yesterday."

"Oh, did you dear? And how did it go?"

"We had a lovely time and we plan to get together over the weekend."

She didn't think it was necessary to tell Mercedes about their personal weekend plans.

"Well Jennifer, I am happy for you. As I mentioned before, he's a lovely young man from a wonderful family and I would be thrilled if it works out for both of you. Now that you have already gotten to know each other, I'm sure he'll invite you to the Red Cross Ball himself. If I don't speak with you before, have a good weekend."

Jennifer was pleased with their conversation, and happy that she had told Mercedes about meeting Javier. Now she had to go about focusing upon her business. She had to start placing the money of the couple whose account she had opened before her lunch date yesterday. Since their primary goal was income, she looked on the firm's fixed income inventory and found a couple of callable CDs along with several investment grade bonds. She then gave them a call to get their permission to purchase the instruments. They appreciated the fact that she had followed up so soon and had heeded their concerns about income and safety of principal. She mentioned that maybe next week might be a good time to purchase some solid dividend paying stocks. They agreed and told her that they looked forward to her call next week. Jennifer then placed the orders on her computer. She was surprised to see that as soon as the orders placed, a tally came up on the screen of the commissions she had earned so far for the day.

Even though Jennifer was beginning to accumulate assets, she could see what an arduous task it was to really earn a living at this business. Happily, she was still on a recruit salary but she knew that would be over by year-end and she was determined to move out of her parents' house to her own apartment sooner than later.

As if on cue, Lowell popped his head into the office. "Jennifer, I see that you've opened a couple of nice sized accounts. There's a $15.00 POSOM yielding 9%, out this month. I'm counting on you to do your share. I strongly suggest that you participate in this offering. It's called: job security."

After making those "encouraging remarks," off he went. Jennifer couldn't help but think what an obnoxious little man he was. But unfortunately, right now, she had no leverage to deal with him. She knew that one day, she would.

Chapter 19

Saturday morning, Jennifer woke up with a smile on her face. She was so looking forward to seeing Javier again. His scent had left an imprint and a desire on her memory.

Before slipping out of her PJ's, she decided to start packing her bag for the adventure date. Her first decision was to select a dress for dinner that night. Drop-dead gorgeous was the prerequisite. After a careful perusal of her wardrobe, Jennifer settled on a hot pink silk jersey Dior sheath. She knew the color exploded next to her blond hair and blue eyes. It was clingy in just the right places; grabbing her curves, without appearing to look cheap. "Sexy" was a compliment that Jennifer abhorred. Elegance had always been her signature. She chose a pair of bronze stiletto Blahnik's and a jeweled Leiber clutch. Since the dress had such a bold color, she decided to wear minimal jewelry; just a pair of diamond drop earrings and gold Rolex. She laid the ensemble on her bed for a final review and was quite pleased with what she had put together. Jennifer felt confident that Javier would be swept away.

She pulled out a Vuitton duffel from the closet shelf that she would fill with her cosmetics and toiletries. For her Sunday outfit, as luck would have it, Jennifer found a pair of tan jodhpurs from last season that she paired with a camel cashmere sweater. A gold and yellow Hermes scarf, a black velvet cap and brown leather short-cut boots completed the look. As a youngster, Jennifer had excelled at dressage, never playing polo, but still, she knew her way around horses and was looking forward to showing off her riding skills to Javier. Since she was packing a bag anyway, she decided to throw in a maillot. Better to be over-prepared.

Now that the packing was complete, Jennifer got dressed for her Saturday morning tennis lesson. It actually was more of a playing session with the club pro, than an actual lesson. Since she had started working in the demanding brokerage business, she wanted to avoid as much stress as possible during her leisure time. So instead of playing competitively on league teams, she opted to pay to play with the pro. After tennis, she would grab a bite at the club and then head back home to prepare for the evening's activities. She was hoping to sneak in a quick nap so she would look refreshed.

The day flew by. Before Jennifer knew it, she was getting dressed for her date. She only had half an hour left before the driver was due at the house. Happily, her parents had left earlier in the day, so they wouldn't be there to ask any more questions. They had planned a dinner cruise on the family yacht with several of their friends and had left in the afternoon to take care of last minute details. As promised, she had given them Javier's name and cell number.

At exactly 6:30, the doorbell rang and the uniformed driver was at the door to whisk Jennifer up to Palm Beach. He helped her into the backseat and stowed her duffel in the trunk. Right behind the driver's seat, Jennifer found a bottle of Dom Perignon chilling in an ice bucket accompanied by two Baccarat flutes. Next to her on the back seat was a single white rose with an envelope lying next to it. She opened the envelope. It read, "Looking forward to our lovely evening together," signed, "With kisses, Javier." Before the driver settled into the car he asked Jennifer if she was ready for the champagne. She accepted his offer, but promised herself just a few sips. She remembered that they were going out for cocktails before dinner and wanted to thoroughly enjoy the evening without the haze of alcohol.

Within 45 minutes, the town car was turning west off A1A onto El Vedado Way. It was a narrow street heading toward Lake Worth. All Jennifer could see were huge manicured hedges obscuring the homes behind them. When they reached the end of the street, the car turned into a gated, cobblestone driveway. Since the sun had just set, Jennifer couldn't clearly see the details of the house. As the car came to a stop, a smiling Javier opened her door. "Darling, thank you so much for coming. I have been looking forward to seeing you all day."

He took her hand and helped her out of the car. The house appeared to have a classic Mediterranean style but with a tropical décor. Javier told the driver that they would be having a drink and would be ready to go to dinner in about an hour. Jennifer noticed how beautifully the home was decorated. The foyer was quite large with a domed ceiling and a fountain in the center. Its walls were curved around the fountain with inserts containing the statues of Greek muses. Javier, still holding Jennifer's hand said, "Jennifer, welcome to my home, may I show you around?"

"Of course, by all means."

Javier led Jennifer through the foyer to the living room. The room had beautiful chairs and couches upholstered with big bold colorful flowered fabrics. Impressionistic styled paintings of the French Riviera adorned the walls along with several large gilded mirrors. They continued walking through to the kitchen which was equipped with two Sub-Zero refrigerators, a large granite covered island with several Viking cooking tops. The kitchen also had a wood burning oven. "Javier, someone in this family likes to cook."

"Actually Jennifer, I'm the one that likes to eat. I have a terrific chef who comes in and my mother, who lives next door, is a wonderful cook. Plus, I do a lot of entertaining with my clients and having them come over to the house adds a personal touch. Here, let me show you the ballroom."

Jennifer had been to a lot of homes in her life but never one with its own ballroom. The room was huge, covered with a yellow canvas roof and inlaid wooden flooring. "Jennifer, my house was originally designed by the famous architect, Addison Mizner, over 70 years ago. In that era, people loved to entertain lavishly at home. The original owner of this house was the heir to a large German pharmaceutical company and they loved to throw lavish parties with a full orchestra so all the guests could dance the waltz. One day I will show you a book I have of the history of the house. It is quite fascinating. I purchased the home about five years ago, completely gutted it but saved the ballroom. It keeps the memory alive of an era gone by. Now I'd like to show you my favorite part of the house."

He opened a door and they walked outside. In front of them was Lake Worth. There was an Olympic size pool with a separate cabana house. "If you don't mind, Jennifer, I thought we would have a cocktail here before going out to dinner?"

"Javier, that's a wonderful idea."

He walked over to the outside wet bar adjoining the cabana house. Jumbo shrimp on ice were awaiting their arrival. "Jennifer, my dear, what may I get you to drink. A martini, Cosmopolitan, glass of wine, whatever you would like."

"Javier, what are you having?"

"I'm having my usual, Glenfilditch on the rocks."

"I'll join you. Make that two." Scotch really was one of Jennifer's favorite cocktails, so she was glad that he suggested it.

Javier scooped several ice cubes into each Baccarat "old-fashioned" glass, then poured the golden elixir of Glenfiddich into the vessels. He handed her a glass and raised his. "Jennifer, to a beautiful evening and to our long lasting relationship together." They clicked glasses and they each took a drink of the aged whiskey. Javier helped Jennifer up to one of the stools encircling the bar, offering her a shrimp. She took it but frankly was too excited to eat. The drink though did slow her down and she began to relax. She let Javier do all the talking. He told her a little more about the house, including the fact that where they were now sitting had originally been the servants' quarters. When the house had been built in the thirties, it was quite common to have a dozen or so servants to take care of the daily chores. In those days there were none of the modern conveniences available now, so everything had to be done by hand. When he bought the house, he razed the building and built the cabana house. It contained a game room as well as a sauna and steam room. On the second floor there was a theatre to entertain guests with first run movies.

Javier took a look at his watch. "Darling, it's 7:45, are you hungry? Let's head over to Café Europe."

Jennifer grabbed her bag and Javier his jacket. The car was waiting for them in the driveway. Javier helped Jennifer in and the driver held the door open for Javier to enter. The bottle of DP was still chilling in the ice bucket. Javier noticed that it had hardly been touched. "Well I guess you don't like my selection of champagne?"

"No," Jennifer said, "I just wanted to arrive lucid and be able to enjoy the evening."

"Since there is so much left, I think we should enjoy a little taste before we get to the restaurant." Javier poured them each half a flute of champagne. Instead of offering a toast, Javier leaned over and gave Jennifer a light kiss on her lips. The kiss and the champagne once again heightened the heat inside Jennifer. As he kissed her, she detected the scent she had been longing for. Even though she felt a pulsating feeling in her crotch, she was determined not to let herself go. With a man like

Javier, she knew that the longer she could put him off sexually the more intrigued he would be. The car stopped in front of the restaurant, the valet opened her door. Javier came around the other side and put his arm around her petite waist, leading her into the restaurant. As they walked in, a pianist was playing Broadway tunes. The owner immediately came over to greet them. "Mr. Cordova, it's so nice to have you join us for dinner this evening."

"Hans, it's great to be here. This is Ms. Palmer and I told her about what a wonderful restaurant you have."

Hans led them to a banquette in a large room decorated with magnificent floral arrangements. Jennifer thought that they were too beautiful to be real. After sitting down in a quiet corner of the room, Javier told her how the owner's wife herself goes down to the flower market each week and selects and styles the floral arrangements. The room was festive and full of happy patrons. The waiter came by with bottled water and menus. "Would you like anything from the bar?"

Javier looked at Jennifer and responded, "We just had drinks, but I'd like to see the wine list." The waiter brought over the wine list. "Now my dear Jennifer, everything on this menu is absolutely delicious. Typically, I start with the grilled fois gras and order the sole amandine. For dessert the pommes tartaine is the best around. But, you take a look."

Jennifer looked at the menu and decided on the selections Javier had suggested. The waiter came over and took their orders. Javier chose a Pouilly Montrachet to accompany the dinner.

After the waiter had left, Javier turned to Jennifer and said, "I m so happy you came up. I have missed you terribly since our luncheon together. Having you by my side makes me feel complete."

Wow, Jennifer thought, this guy is not playing games and he seems so sincere. How refreshing.

While they were eating their appetizer, Javier asked Jennifer how she likes the business of money management. She told him that even though the world markets were going through challenging times, she enjoyed her career. She did mention the difficulty of accomplishing true success as an honest broker. "Honestly, Javier, it seems as though the brokers that really care about the clients' assets lose, as opposed to those who could care less and are just looking for the big bucks for themselves. You would cringe at the stories I could tell you about what goes on in the office. Plus, the big firms perpetuate it. They are in the business to make money. Period! It can be very frustrating, especially when you have been at the top of your game in all your endeavors. And suddenly, by being honest, you find yourself on the bottom rung."

She really didn't want to admit to him yet that she was just starting out because she didn't want Mercedes to know what a novice she was.

"Jennifer, I started out in a hedge fund and I have an inkling of what you are saying. But now that I have my own firm, I'm able to play by my own rules. And happily, my returns have been in the highest percentile of my peers. Maybe, down the road, Tate and Yardley, through your introduction, might be able to take advantage of our services for your clients. But, let's not discuss business. Tonight is about you and me getting to know each other better."

The waiter came by the table, opening and pouring the wine into their glasses. Several minutes later he returned with a large platter containing the sole. Tableside, he deboned the dish and served it to them, accompanied with sautéed new potatoes and baby carrots. Javier was right, the food was delicious.

During dinner, Javier told Jennifer more about his background. He spoke about how much he loved and respected his family. "Jennifer, I just know my parents would adore you. Hopefully when they come up for the holidays, they will have the privilege of meeting you."

After they had finished their meal, the waiter cleared the table in preparation for the soufflé. Before the dessert arrived, Javier grasped both of Jennifer's hands. "My darling, being with you this evening has exceeded my highest expectations. Our time together seems so effortless and natural. You look so beautiful." He then moved forward and gave Jennifer a long, luscious kiss on her lips. She returned his kiss with equal passion. They were interrupted by the waiter carrying a serving dish of tarte tartaine. He served it to them with a generous portion of crème Anglaise. While they both were savoring the sweet delicacy, Javier said, "O.K. now it's your choice, we can go over to Taboo for an after dinner drinks or back to my house. What would you like to do, Jennifer?"

Jennifer would have loved to go back to his home. Javier was simply irresistible to her. She could only imagine how he would make love to her. But she also was determined not to let things get out of hand on their first date. Javier was definitely the kind of guy who was used to getting things his way. Even though Jennifer hated playing games, she knew that in the long run that by being elusive she would maintain his attention. "Let's go to Taboo. Maybe they'll have music tonight and we can work off some of this wonderful dinner."

Javier paid the bill, helped Jennifer out of the banquette and they walked out of the restaurant hand in hand. The car was waiting for them. After they got in, Javier put his arm around Jennifer and kissed her again. This time not just on her lips but around her ears and down her neck. He looked up at the driver and quickly said, "Let's head to Taboo." Not missing a beat, he squeezed Jennifer closer to him. She could feel the warmth of his breath and was again intoxicated by his scent. He had certainly mastered the art of seduction. And it felt so good to Jennifer to be in a man's arms. He took her hand and placed it on his crotch. It was stone hard. "You see what you do to me?"

Jennifer couldn't stop returning his kisses. Before they knew it, the car had pulled up in front of Taboo and the driver was holding the door open. Quickly, Jennifer got hold of herself, reapplied her lipstick, and was good to go.

The restaurant was buzzing. The season was just about to roll into full swing and with the early frost up north, the snowbirds had flocked down to their winter homes. The great thing about Taboo was that it attracted a diverse group of guests. There were women in evening gowns with men in tuxedoes apparently bored with whatever fundraiser they had attended. There were college kids in polo shirts and jeans just looking for a good time and of course the wannabes: the men and women from off the island looking to land a wealthy date. The eclectic mix created electricity in the room. As Jennifer and Javier made their way to the back of the restaurant, Jennifer heard someone calling Javier's name. She turned around and saw that it was Mercedes. She saw Javier go over to her and give her a kiss on the mouth. Jennifer was a little surprised since his lips had just been passionately kissing hers. But, she knew they were very good friends. And maybe, she reasoned, this was the way very good friends greeted each other. When Mercedes saw Jennifer, she got up and brought her over to the table. "I'm so happy to see you both here. What a surprise! Come, join us. I've ordered champagne."

Javier glanced at Jennifer as if to ask if she minded. Jennifer said, "Great, we'd love to join you."

As they sat down at the table, Mercedes introduced them to her friends. They were two older couples, all were attired formally. "We're playing hooky from the Diabetes Ball. It just got so boring, terrible food and music. Can you believe they charged $500 a ticket and they didn't even have a live orchestra? Just a DJ. I mean really, one can only take so much."

Jennifer detected a slight slur in Mercedes' words. It sounded as though she'd had a bit too much to drink. But despite that, she still looked grand in her purple gown with a deep décolletage. Jennifer noticed her jewelry. Big diamond earrings with a matching necklace. Only Mercedes could elegantly pull off such a bold look. The champagne arrived and Mercedes stood up. "I'd like to toast my friends and especially, my new friend Jennifer." She took a sip and grabbed Javier's hand, saying, "Come dance with me."

Jennifer sat at the table with her friends making small talk, but still glancing up to watch Javier and Mercedes dance. Even though the music was fast, they were dancing close together, speaking into each other's ear. The room was loud, so Jennifer assumed that was the only way they could communicate. After the song was over, they came back and Javier extended his hand to Jennifer. She happily took it and off they went to the dance floor. He held her body close to him. She could feel his hardness rubbing over her body. She knew he was hot and she was only getting hotter. Thank God they hadn't gone back to his place. While dancing to a few more songs, Jennifer caught Mercedes staring at them. She couldn't imagine her being jealous. Most likely, the alcohol was just sinking in to her system. After their fourth dance, Javier turned to Jennifer and said, "Are you ready to go? I have a big day planned for us tomorrow."

Jennifer nodded her head and they went back to the table to bid Mercedes and her friends adieu. As they got back into the waiting car, Javier couldn't wait to continue where he had left off; kissing Jennifer's neck and face. As he came up for air, he said, "One final choice for the evening, The Brazilian Court or my house?"

Jennifer looked at him and gave him a sensuous kiss on his lips and then sat back. Reluctantly she said, "I think it best for both of us that you drop me off at the hotel. After all, we have all day tomorrow together."

Javier directed the driver to head to the hotel and again grabbed Jennifer, kissing her and saying, "You drive me wild."

He didn't know what wild was; Jennifer thought she'd have an orgasm right there, in the back seat of the car.

The car pulled up to the front of the hotel. A bellman came out to retrieve Jennifer's luggage. "You're all checked in. It's room #222. Would you like me to walk you to your room?"

Jennifer smiled as she stepped out of the car. "I think it best if we say our good-byes here. For both our sakes."

"In that case," Javier said, "have pleasant dreams and I'll be by to pick you up tomorrow at 10:00 a.m. We'll go for a horseback ride and then I've planned a picnic lunch."

They both looked at each other and fell into one more passionate embrace. Jennifer said, "Let me go, so I can get my beauty sleep for tomorrow. Thank you for a beautiful evening."

Jennifer followed the bellman to her room. When he opened the door, she was pleasantly surprised to discover that Javier had reserved a suite for her. She recalled that the Brazilian Court had been built nearly half a century ago and had just undergone a major renovation. The bellman set her luggage down and asked her if she would need anything else? She told him she was fine and he bid her a good night. Jennifer went into the bathroom and gazed at herself in the mirror. Her face was flushed and she looked a bit disheveled. She wanted to take a shower before going to bed but chose not to in order to savor the scent of Javier on her body. She slowly undressed and recalled in detail the evening's events. As she slipped between the cool sheets of the bed she played over in her mind Javier's lips touching hers, his tongue darting in and out of her mouth, the way he fondled her breasts. She couldn't stop thinking of his firm penis rubbing up against her body while they danced. She eventually fell asleep hugging the pillow next to her.

Chapter 20

Jennifer was in a deep sleep when she heard the phone ringing. Groggily, she picked up the receiver. "Darling Jennifer, I trust you had a wonderful sleep. It's 9:30 a.m.; I'll pick you up in half an hour. We'll have a light breakfast and then head over to the stables. Is that all right with you?"

"Javier, I'm still in bed, could you please give me an hour? You go have breakfast and pick me up when you finish."

"Darling, It's fine with me, I just wish I were next to you right now. But, since I'm not, I'll see you in exactly one hour. I couldn't bear to wait a minute longer."

"Me too, Javier. I'll see you then." After they hung up Jennifer jumped out of bed and headed straight to the shower. Within 45 minutes, she had gotten dressed, packed up her clothes from the night before and was heading to the lobby to meet Javier. Before leaving the room, she took a glance at herself and was quite pleased with her refection. The tan colored outfit she was wearing with the jodhpurs and riding boots was striking. She hoped Javier would be equally impressed. As she walked into the lobby, she spotted Javier; his back was turned towards her. He was reading the *New York Times.* As if on cue, he turned around and displayed his gorgeous smile. He looked as though he had just stepped out of a Ralph Lauren ad, handsome in a pink polo shirt and white riding pants tucked into his polo boots. He had a purple cashmere sweater tied around his neck.

Javier reached out to Jennifer and pulled her close to him. Hugging her, he whispered in her ear, "You look beautiful. I missed you desperately." They walked out to a white convertible Porsche Carrera parked in the driveway with its top down. He helped Jennifer into the car, got into the driver's seat and off they went to the polo grounds.

When they pulled up to the stables, there were two polo ponies that had been saddled up by the groomsman. Jennifer noticed how beautiful the ponies were; caramel in color and perfectly brushed out. Javier helped her get on her horse and he then got on to his. "Are you ready for a trot? Follow me." Before Jennifer knew it, Javier had taken off like lightning. She was determined not to let him show her up, quickly catching up to him.

"Jennifer, you are doing a great job. I don't think that this is your first time on a horse. Just be prepared, these are polo ponies, they are used to speed." He picked up the pace and Jennifer kept up. After riding for almost an hour, Javier led them to a clearing that had been set up for a picnic lunch. There was a thick plaid blanket laid out on the forest floor. On it was an ice bucket filled with a bottle of wine, a selection of paninis, grapes, shiny apples and a platter laden with a variety of cookies. Jennifer felt as though she were dreaming. She couldn't believe how romantic Javier was. He must really like her to have gone to all this trouble.

Javier got off his horse first and tied it to the nearest tree. He then walked over to Jennifer and held out his hands to help her. As her feet touched the ground, she fell into his arms. They kissed and held each other. Jennifer felt the now familiar hardness of his penis rub against her. His lust for her was contagious. She desired him as much as he wanted her. She knew that even though it was almost impossible to resist him, she would have to persist in putting him off.

"Javier, this looks like a scene out of a movie. How creative you are to put this together, plus, I'm absolutely starving."

"Jennifer, I'm absolutely starving also." He again grabbed her body in his arms and gently lowered her onto the blanket, passionately kissing her. She adored the taste of his mouth and running her fingers through his thick hair. But the voice inside of her said to put the brakes on. She gently pushed him away.

"Javier, we can't let all these foods go to waste. I'd love a glass of wine." He poured the Chardonnay into crystal wineglasses for both of them.

He held his glass up. "Jennifer, I am crazy about you. Thank you for stepping into my life." They each took a sip and once again he started to passionately kiss her face and neck. Eventually, Jennifer, despite herself, was able to get him to settle down and consume the gourmet delights. "Jennifer, I want you to know how much I have enjoyed spending time with you. I am dreading having to drive you home later this afternoon. You know, Mercedes has taken a couple of tables for the Red Cross Ball, and I would be honored for you to join me. It's in two weeks, can you make it?"

Jennifer didn't want to reveal to him that Mercedes had already planned for them to come together all along. "Javier, that sounds great. I'd love to. Shall we have a bite of this lovely picnic you put together for us?" She then reached out for a panini, hoping that the distraction of lunch would settle Javier's libido down. Happily, he was also famished. After taking a few bites, Jennifer said, "Alfresco dining always heightens my appetite."

Javier responded, "Jennifer, only you heighten my appetite, but I get the message. Please accept my apologies for coming on so strongly.

I'm just so attracted to you. I promise to behave. Now, I'll try to be serious. Tell me, how are you dealing with the challenges of your business?"

"I try to do the very best for my clients, but of course I know that I can't control the markets. It's very difficult to operate in an environment where all the variables are literally out of your hands. Especially when you care about your clients." She still didn't want him to know that she was for now merely a trainee.

"Jennifer, I can understand what you are saying. We have been quite fortunate at my firm. With the logarithms we've developed, the performance for our clients' accounts has been consistently stellar. They have a chance to liquidate their holdings twice a year and we have just passed the second yearly redemption period. So far, even with the choppy markets, everyone is staying the course. I am very grateful for this. I know they appreciate what we are doing for them. Perhaps, I might be able to relieve you of the anxiety you are sharing with me about your business. We would be happy to open the door for you to refer your clients to us. That way, you would receive a handsome fee, reduce your level of frustration and best of all your clients would be making money in good times as well as bad. It's a win-win situation for everyone. You know, Jennifer, typically our minimum account investment is $10 million, but because of our relationship, I could lower it to $500,000. What do you think of that idea, my darling?" He picked up her hand and kissed it.

"Javier, I am flattered that you would want to help me in my business. The only catch is that I am employed by Tate and Yardley, and I signed an agreement that I couldn't place my clients' funds with any outside managers unless they are part of the Tate Yardley network."

"My darling, that is no problem at all. I will give you all the information in writing about myself and Cordova Investments. You can present it to your firm and I have no doubt they will add it to their menu of portfolio managers. I will even give you a list of our clients as well as testimonials. Once we receive your firm's approval, you will be able to move forward, freeing yourself from any anxiety and having the ability to earn a handsome living."

Jennifer was excited by his proposition. She recalled what she had read about his firm and how he had outperformed all his peers, becoming *Forbes*, Portfolio Manager of the Year. All she would have to do is find the clients and just hand them over to Javier. The best part is that she would be getting paid for it without really having any responsibility. He was right. It was indeed a win-win proposition. She just had to get it approved by Tate Yardley. This would be her pathway to becoming a "big producer." Once everything was in place she would have Lowell eating out of her hand.

Javier interrupted her thoughts by kissing her on the lips and popping a firm, juicy grape into her mouth with his tongue. Once again, he laid her back down on the blanket and kissed her on the mouth with long sensuous kisses. She was so physically excited by him and mentally excited by his business proposition that it became difficult to delay his sexual overtures. She adored being with him and the sexual attraction they shared for each other was overwhelming. They continued to roll around on the blanket passionately kissing each other. She felt his hand gently grabbing onto her breasts. It then slowly moved down her chest, making its way between her legs. His touch felt so good. She could have easily have moved on but thank God she was wearing pants. Jennifer knew though, that things were on the cusp of heading to the point of no return. She gently took his hand and placed it on her cheek. "Javier, I want you as much as you want me. But I think it's best for both of us to take a 'time out.' Sometimes, the better things in life are worth waiting for." She leaned over and gave him a luscious French kiss.

"Jennifer, being with you gives me completion. To me LOVE is a very special word. To be used on rare occasions if at all. But Jennifer, I love every part of you."

Jennifer was taken off guard with his proclamation. She felt love for him as well but felt it best to wait. She was afraid to show her hand so early in their relationship. She had been hurt far too many times. But something inside her gave her the feeling that this was the real thing. She could see spending the rest of her life with Javier. Instead of speaking, she reached out to him, hugging and kissing him. "Javier, your words mean so much to me. This is has been one of the most memorable moments of my life."

They continued kissing until they noticed that the sun had started to fade. Javier looked at his watch. "I can't believe it's almost 5:00. Let's head back to the stables, drop off the ponies and then I'll sadly drive you back home."

"Javier, what about all this food? How do we pack it up?"

"Not to worry, my darling. I'll phone my housekeeper and she will bring everything back to the house."

They reluctantly climbed back onto their ponies and trotted back to the stables. Jennifer's horse out sped Javier's. Her pony was definitely on a mission to get back to the stables. The wind against her face cooled down her body heat. Once back at the stables, the groomsman assisted the couple in getting off their ponies and took the horses back to the stalls for a bath and a well-deserved meal.

Little was said on the drive back to Miami. The convertible top was down. And it seemed as though the air was sobering them up. Javier held her hand tightly all the way down. When they arrived at her exit and were stopped at a traffic light, he leaned over and kissed her. Jennifer was thinking about how fortunate she was to have met such a quality man like Javier. He had so much to offer and seemed to genuinely care for her. His consideration towards her was over the top. She couldn't wait to see him again.

Within moments, they had arrived in front of her parents' home. Javier got out and gathered her luggage. She noticed that he also had taken a large envelope out of the trunk of the car. They walked to the front door together, arm in arm. "Jennifer, next week, I'll come down here, check into the Mandarin on Saturday and this time you will plan the weekend. How does that sound? Also, here is all the information your company may need to do the proper due diligence on Cordova Investments."

Jennifer thought it a bit odd that he carried information regarding his company in the trunk of his car. But he was the owner and CEO after all. Better to be prepared.

"Javier, I can't wait. It will be difficult to compete with the last 24 hours, but I already have a few ideas. Do you play tennis?"

"But, of course."

"OK, bring your racket. Whatever we do, I know we will have a great time. Thank you for a lovely weekend. I really appreciate all the thought you put into it."

Javier pulled her toward him. "My bellissima, I will be thinking of you every moment of the day. And thank you for coming up to Palm Beach. I will phone you tomorrow and will think about you every moment of the day."

He then proceeded to give her a delicious French kiss and a hug. As he turned away and walked toward his car, Jennifer waited by the door to see if he would turn around. He did and mouthed the words, "I love you." She blew him a kiss and opened the door to the house.

Chapter 21

Jennifer got to the office bright and early Monday morning. She was happy to see Lowell's car parked in the garage. She knew that if she didn't get to him first thing, she'd have a long wait. After placing her case and Journal on her desk, she made a beeline straight to his office. Happily, Estelle, his gatekeeper had yet to arrive. As she approached his doorway, she saw that he was reading the *Wall Street Journal* but glanced up, "Good morning, Jennifer, what's up?" One thing predictable about Lowell was that he didn't mince words and cut to the chase. He was only interested in any conversation if it had a direct positive monetary impact on him. Clearly, Jennifer had an inkling that this conversation would. Without his invitation, she strode into his office and took a seat on the couch situated beside his desk.

"You know, Lowell; something came up this weekend that I believe can be mutually beneficial to us and Tate Yardley." She noticed that she had his attention. She went on to tell him about the Cordova group and about how she had met the owner and principal of the company. She further discussed the fact of their track record and how they had become the "darling" of Wall Street. She discussed the offer that was made to her regarding the fee for referrals, and how Lowell as well as Tate Yardley could capitalize on the relationship. Needless to say, Lowell appeared intrigued. He was even taking notes.

"Jennifer, it sounds good to me, but you know that we work for a large firm and they need to endorse this Cordova Group before we can approach our clients with it."

"Lowell, this envelope should have everything the firm needs. So what it is the next step?"

"I'll overnight these papers up to the home office and we should have an answer by weekend. Jennifer, I appreciate you bringing this to my attention. As the introducing manager of a new product to the firm, once accepted by corporate, our branch will get an override on all the business done with this one manager firm wide. I will let you know as soon as I hear back from headquarters." He then went back to reading his paper. Jennifer knew him well enough by now to assume she was dismissed. Walking back to her office, Jennifer felt that if having Cordova managers approved by the firm would directly affect Lowell's wallet, he would do whatever humanly possible to get the job done.

As she reached her desk, the phone was ringing, and she saw Cordova Investments on the Caller ID. Her heart skipped a beat as she picked up the receiver. "Javier, is that you?"

"My darling angel, I have spent all night thinking of you. I couldn't wait to phone and hear the sound of your voice. I was planning on leaving a voicemail for you because I didn't think you would be in the office so early."

"Javier, it's so good to hear from you. And yes, I miss you also. I came in early today to speak with my manager about our business relationship."

"Tell me, Jennifer, what did he say?'

"Well, I gave him your written material and he seemed to be excited about the proposition. But he also told me that it has to be approved by our home office. He felt fairly certain that there wouldn't be an issue. Between you and me, anything that affects his net worth makes him happy. He said that we should know something by Friday."

"Jennifer, I'm in town all week. If they need anything at all to complete their due diligence, I am available. If need be, I am happy to fly up to New York to meet with them. If we get the go ahead this week, we can celebrate together Saturday night. I have a meeting in a few minutes, will phone you again soon. Remember my darling, I love you."

Wow, what a way to start the day, Jennifer thought.

The week was busy; Jennifer had several more appointments with prospective clients that had all responded to her written solicitation. Tuesday, she received notification that all of Mercedes' account assets were in her account at Tate Yardley. Jennifer was looking forward to reviewing the positions and putting together a viable plan for Mercedes. Her goal was to complete it by Thursday and phone her with an action plan. Coincidentally, Tuesday's mail delivered Mercedes' invitation to the Red Cross Ball. She noticed that the requested dress code was white tie. She had only nine days left to buy a gown. Since Javier was coming to Miami this weekend, she planned to go to Bal Harbor Friday night and check out Neiman's and Saks.

Thursday, she had to attend the requisite "sales meeting." Once again, Lowell drove home the fact that the office was almost on track to achieve his year-end goal with the ultimate prize being a year-end dinner party. Apparently, this was a motivating factor to many of the brokers in the office. He then posted the monthly production list as an addendum to the daily list of brokers' commissions. Of course, the usual suspects were at the top of the list. Jennifer had mixed emotions, on the one hand she detested it, and didn't want the others to know her business. She felt that the "churners and burners" always made the top ten. But still, she had something to prove. She was a winner and she knew it, but she wasn't going to blatantly take advantage of her innocent clients. Instead, she would eventually put the whole lot of them to shame. She would handle her clients' assets with the respect they deserved. She would place their assets with one of the top money managers in the country.

After the meeting was finished, she heard Lowell's squeaky voice calling out her name. "Jennifer, I need to have a word with you. I'll be in my office in a couple of minutes. Meet you there." Jennifer felt a tinge of excitement. He probably had heard from upper management concerning Cordova Investments. She practically sprinted to his office. Per usual, in typical Lowell fashion, she was kept waiting for ten minutes. When he finally appeared, he closed the door and sat behind his desk. "Jennifer, as you know, I sent the information regarding Cordova Investments up to our Managed Portfolio Division. I just received a call this morning from the head of the Due Diligence committee. Apparently their investigation of Cordova Investments resulted in a couple of red flags. So the end result is that Tate Yardley prohibits you from placing client assets with Cordova."

Jennifer was confused. "What do you mean by red flags? This company was lauded by *Forbes* as the Portfolio Manager of the year. Lowell, there must be some mistake."

"Look, Jennifer, they didn't give me any specifics. All I can tell you is that, after this report, dealing with them is a direct violation of firm policy which could result in your termination. I see that you are starting to open accounts and attract assets. Drop Cordova Investments."

"But Lowell is there anything we can do to change their minds? I know the principal is more than happy to fly up to New York and meet with the committee."

"Jennifer, as far as I'm concerned, he can stand on his head. The answer is no. It would be a feather in their cap to be aligned with Tate Yardley and apparently Cordova doesn't suit the requirements necessary to be accepted by our firm. Young lady, I strongly suggest you move on. As a broker just starting out your career, you can't afford to screw up. Now, I have work to do."

Jennifer could barely stand up and head out of the room. As she walked to her office, she felt as though her balloon had just been deflated. What could the "red flags" be? Surely they were mistaken. She was sure that Javier could straighten things out. When she finally sat down at her desk, she picked up the phone to call Javier. But something stopped her. Maybe it was better to tell him in person. After all, they would be together over the weekend. She was totally frustrated with the firm. With all the garbage products they encourage the brokers to sell to their clients, how dare they make a judgment call about Cordova Investments? Jennifer was seething but knew that she had to get over it, at least for now. She had to distract herself from this utter lunacy. This was as good a time as any to call Mercedes and discuss her account.

She dialed her number and Mercedes cheerfully answered the phone. Jennifer was happy that at least she was in a good mood. They discussed Jennifer's ideas for the account and Mercedes gave her the go ahead to do whatever she felt was best. "Jennifer, I honestly trust you. You know your business far better than me. I have full faith that you will do right by me. Now, let's talk up Mr. Cordova. It was great seeing you both together last weekend. You make a striking couple. Do you like him?"

"Mercedes, he's a great guy. He really has it all. I can't possibly thank you enough for introducing us. He invited me to the ball; I'm looking forward to it. You really couldn't have planned it out any better."

Jennifer was holding back. She didn't want to tell Mercedes that she had stayed over through Sunday or that Javier was coming down this weekend. True, she was a client as well as a friend, but Jennifer kept recalling the look in Mercedes' eyes when she and Javier were dancing. She felt it best to keep the conversation light. It was better than creating an animosity and shooting herself in the foot.

"Well, my dear, you know what they say about the best laid plans...now I must run, my masseur will be here in five minutes. If we don't speak before, I can't wait to see you at the ball. And regarding my account, I know you'll do the right thing. Love and kisses dear, talk with you soon."

Jennifer was pleased with their conversation. Mercedes had literally given her carte blanche over the account. At least it helped to dull her earlier disappointment about Tate Yardley's decision.

Jennifer noticed that there was 15 minutes left to the closing bell and just like the Energizer Bunny, she saw Lowell running around to each broker encouraging them to get their tickets in for the day, so more revenues would be generated. Watching him made her think about how much she had looked forward to elevating herself from this mediocrity. She knew in her soul that Javier would come through with a solution.

Chapter 22

Friday afternoon, immediately after the close, Jennifer was off to the Bal Harbor Shoppes with the mission of finding a gown for the Red Cross Ball. She was looking forward to the drive up. It would give her a chance to sort out her thoughts before seeing Javier the next day. She still couldn't believe that Tate Yardley had blocked her from referring clients to Cordova Investments. She was annoyed with them, but at the same time, wondered what the "red flags" really meant. She was confident that Javier could explain everything to her and the firm so she could move forward. She had been so distracted that she hadn't even made any plans for the weekend. During the drive, she thought it might be fun to have dinner on Calle Ocho on Saturday night. She knew of a great Castilian restaurant that made the best Arroz con Mariscos. Javier would definitely enjoy the tapas, some sangria and a great main course. Maybe after dinner they would stop by one of the Spanish cabarets and dance the night away. On Sunday, they would go to the club, play tennis and have lunch at the clubhouse. After lunch, they might take a bike ride through the Grove. Hopefully the weather would cooperate. Jennifer turned into the parking lot and found a spot right by Saks.

Maybe that was a good omen. She headed straight up to the designer department on the second floor. She knew what she wanted, something elegant but a little edgy.

A red gown caught her attention at the Valentino boutique. It was a sleeveless silk jersey with a fishtail hem. She was compelled to try it on. Amazingly it was her size. The front had a high neckline accentuating her long neck and the back was drop dead gorgeous, it was cut low, just short of the rise on her buttocks. The dress looked as though it was made for her. All it needed was a slight tapering around her tiny waist. Jennifer was so thrilled that she conveniently forgot to look at the price tag. While disrobing in the dressing room she gasped when she saw that it was $4,500. She knew that this ball was "the" ball of the Palm Beach season and being with Javier and sitting at Mercedes' table, she had to look terrific. She also knew that she was currently earning next to nothing, but she reasoned that her luck was changing and buying the dress was an investment in her future. She would take the money out of her trust fund and as soon as she could, would replace it. After all, she had to have that dress. When the saleswoman asked her about her decision, she told her that she would purchase the dress if there would be no charge for alterations and that she would receive it before next Wednesday. The saleswoman started to protest, but obviously figured out quickly, that with business so slow, it was in her best interest to please her client. "All right Miss Palmer, as you wish. The dress will be delivered to you no later than Wednesday." Jennifer walked out of the store overjoyed. She had found the perfect gown. She headed home, looking forward to a quiet evening and a good night's sleep. She wanted to look radiant for Javier tomorrow.

Chapter 23

At breakfast the next morning, Jennifer informed her parents about her plans for the weekend. Her mother asked, "Is this the same young man you visited in Palm Beach last week?"

"Yes Mother. He is a great guy and I can't wait to see him this evening."

"Jennifer, we have plans to go out tonight, but why don't you invite him over for a cocktail before we go our separate ways. I'll have Milidia make a couple of hors d'oevres. It seems as though you are quite fond of him and it would be nice for us to meet."

"OK, Mother, when he calls to let me know that he's in town, I'll set it up." Jennifer wasn't quite prepared to introduce Javier to her parents this evening. She really wanted to speak with him as soon as possible about the Cordova Investments situation. But her parents had been so supportive of her over the past few months, that introducing them to Javier was the least she could do. She just didn't want him to get the idea that she was serious about him, so early in their relationship.

She spent the day just hanging around the house. Usually she would have been out and about, but she just wasn't in the mood. She was looking forward to seeing Javier and figuring out how to resolve Tate Yardley's reluctance to doing business with Cordova. At 3:00, her cell phone rang, it was Javier. "Mi amor, I'm here. When can I see you?"

"Javier, I'm so happy to hear from you, you have no idea. My parents thought it would be nice to meet you, so how about coming by the house around 6:30?"

Mi amor, the next three hours will be a lifetime without seeing you. But I will be at your home at 6:30, as you wish and look forward to meeting your parents. Until then, I love you my darling."

Promptly at 6:30, the doorbell rang and Jennifer ran to open the door. Since the evening would be more casual with a Spanish flair, she was wearing a black and red Tse Tse cashmere skirt and top. Her hair was pulled up in a loose chignon, to draw attention to her big, gold hoop earrings. When she opened the door, Javier was standing there with a bottle of wine in one hand and a dozen white roses in the other. He looked so seductive, in a beige jacket with light colored pants and a navy colored shirt, that she couldn't help herself, throwing her arms around his neck and drawing her body close to his. She couldn't get the image of him in the polo pants on his horse out of her mind.

Stepping back, he said, "Mi amor, you look delicious. I brought the roses for you and the wine for your parents."

Jennifer took his arm, walking him through the foyer and over to the bar where her parents were sitting. "Javier, I'd like you to meet my parents."

Her father got up and extended his hand to Javier. "Javier, it's a pleasure to meet you."

"Dr. Palmer, it is my true pleasure to meet the parents of beautiful Jennifer."

He stooped down and gave her mother a kiss on her extended hand.

"So Javier, what may I get you to drink?" her father asked.

"Sir, a glass of white wine would be superb."

Jennifer's father opened a bottle of Kendall Jackson and Milidia brought out stuffed mushrooms and smoked salmon canapés. Dr. Palmer poured a glass of white wine for each of them. After he sat down, Javier said, "It would be an honor for me to make a toast to you both for creating such a magnificent daughter as your Jennifer."

While they touched glasses, Jennifer noticed her mother subtly rolling her eyes, but still managing a smile. They made small talk for about half an hour after which her mother arose. "I hate to break this party up, but your father and I have dinner arrangements with the Atkins' tonight; so nice to meet you, Javier, looking forward to seeing you again."

Jennifer's dad promptly followed suit, extending his hand once again to Javier. "Please stay and finish the bottle of wine and Javier, I trust that you'll take good care of my little girl tonight?"

Javier stood up and again gave her mother a kiss on both cheeks and told her father, "Dr. Palmer, your daughter is most precious to me. Not to worry."

Jennifer saw her parents out to the garage to bid them good-bye and also detect their reaction to Javier. They kissed her but neither made a comment about Javier. She assumed that they were just pre-occupied with getting on their way.

She walked back to the bar where Javier was sipping from his wine glass. "Jennifer, I am so pleased to have met your parents. Not surprising, they are lovely people."

Jennifer was happy that everyone had gotten along so well, but was anxious to speak with Javier about Tate Yardley and his company. When she sat back down at the bar, he took her face in his hands and gave her a long, sensuous kiss. She could smell his familiar scent and taste the sweetness of his mouth. He was irresistible, but she knew they had to talk.

"Javier, I was waiting to see you in person, to tell you that Tate Yardley is prohibiting me from referring my clients to you. They told me that while they were doing due diligence on your company a couple of 'red flags' came up. Javier, what does that mean? What red flags could possibly come up with a company like yours? What can you do to resurrect this idea? I'm at a loss of what to do."

"My darling, Jennifer, I have not the slightest idea of what they mean by red flags. You know me; my company makes money for our clients, period. I will not beg your company to take us on. It's their loss. As they say, there is more than one way to skin a cat. I have to admit to you, that I know that you are just starting out in the business. Since you are not experienced, you need a money manager that will take good care of your clients. With your beauty and my brains, we can take Palm Beach by storm. No worries, I will not tell Mercedes that you are new in the business. In fact, she's just crazy about you. I just want to help you and despite what Tate Yardley says, we can still arrange for you to refer your clients to my company."

"But Javier, you don't understand, the greedy little manager of my office told me that if I place my clients money with you, I could be fired. I'm just starting out in my career; I can't afford to have a black mark against me or even worse."

"Darling Jennifer, I have it all worked out. You will find clients for Cordova Investments and instead of paying you a referral fee I will have our trades, under a different corporate name flow through you at Tate Yardley. So, technically, you won't be earning money for the referrals, nor will you or Tate Yardley have any liability. But my sweetness, you will be earning commissions on the trades we direct through to you. I tell you, after a month of trading activity, your weasel of a manager will be so happy with the revenues you are bringing in that he will conveniently turn the other cheek. You should actually be thankful that Tate Yardley turned us down. This will work out even better for you. Now, mi amor, how does that sound?"

Jennifer just knew that Javier would come up with a solution. If she really wasn't getting paid a referral fee from them and just executing their trades, she was working within the confines of the firm's parameters. What a great idea! She reached out to Javier. "I have been so upset by this, but just knew that you'd figure it out."

He stood and helped her up out of her chair. They hugged and French-kissed, rubbing their warm bodies against each other. Jennifer felt his erection rubbing against her. She could feel the wetness developing in her panties. She knew that no matter how much she wanted him, this was not going to be the night to succumb to his raw sensuality. She wasn't in the mood to offer her parents any explanations. Her plan was to wait until next weekend when she was in Palm Beach.

Milidia came into the room to see if they needed anything, startling Javier. Jennifer suggested they head out for the evening. Javier thanked Milidia in Spanish for her hospitality, Jennifer noticed, charming the socks off of her. They walked outside to his Porsche and headed over to Calle Oucho. Jennifer could tell how pleased Javier was with the plans she had made for dinner. He told her, "I haven't had decent paella in the States except for my mother's. This will be a real treat." They arrived at Bodegon de Castillo and were taken to a table near the open kitchen where they could watch the food being prepared. They started with white sangria and a variety of tapas, both ordering the arroz de mariscos, which was paella containing only seafood. The meal was delicious. While eating their main course a guitarist came over to the table and sang Spanish love ballads to them. They finished their meal with the classic flan drenched in caramel sauce. Javier held Jennifer's hand throughout the whole evening except when they were eating.

After polishing off the pitcher of sangria, Jennifer suggested going over to a nearby cabaret that had an outstanding Flamenco show. The cabaret was just a block away, so they walked over arm in arm. Javier stopped them in their path every few steps to kiss her. When they arrived at the cabaret, they secured a front table. Javier ordered two glasses of Aguardiente. Jennifer had never heard of this drink. Javier explained to her that it came from Colombia and its literal translation was "fire water" and it packed a punch. "So, mi amor, sip it slowly."

The flamenco show was loud and uplifting, the lead male dancer even came into the audience to dance with Jennifer. At first, she was a little hesitant about dancing flamenco, but with Javier's urging and the Aguardiente kicking into her brain, she got into the swing of things and was applauded by the audience. At about 1:00, after dancing together after the show she mentioned to Javier that they might think about leaving. "I have a full day planned for us and don't want to see any sleepyheads."

Javier paid the bill and took Jennifer's hand, leading her out of the club. As they walked to the car he quietly asked, "Jennifer, I have a beautiful suite at The Mandarin, it would be such a pity to have it go to waste just on me. Why don't you join me tonight?"

If he only had a clue about how much Jennifer was longing for him. But she knew that she had to stick to her guns. "Javier, I'm sure it's beautiful, but tonight you'll have to enjoy it alone. We have a lot more fun ahead of us tomorrow and you, my darling boy, need to get a good night's sleep."

"But, mi corazon..."

"No buts tonight, trust me it's better this way."

Javier drove her home and they ended up making out for almost an hour in his car in front of her house. She never realized how inconvenient a stick shift could be. Between the sangria at dinner and the Aguardiente afterwards, her inhibitions were almost dissipated. She did have the wherewithal to finally get out of the car and kiss him goodnight. He walked her to the front door and left her with one more passionate embrace.

"Until tomorrow, mi amor. What time should I pick you up in the morning?"

"How about ten and wear your tennis clothes." Jennifer walked in the house and took one last look at Javier getting in the car and pulling away, before closing the door. Even though her head was cloudy from all the alcohol she had consumed, she knew Javier had had a good time. The evening had come together even better than she had expected. The best part was that the shadow that had preoccupied her thoughts the last few days had vanished. His idea of her referring clients to him away from Tate Yardley and not earning a finders' fee was ingenious. He was right, neither she nor the firm were exposed to any liability. He would simply open up a corporate account and reciprocate the referrals by directing trades her way.

After Jennifer had changed into her pajamas, she was able to finally have a peaceful night's sleep, looking forward to tomorrow's new adventures.

Chapter 24

Despite an atrocious hangover, Jennifer managed to wake up at 8:30. She was anxious to hear what her parents' impression was of Javier and she also wanted to allot enough time to get ready for the day's activities.

Before even changing out of her pajamas, Jennifer ran down the steps to the breakfast room where her parents were eating and reading the Sunday *Times*. When she walked into the room, they both greeted her. She noticed that their responses to her appeared a bit cool. Jennifer had a great relationship with her parents and could tell within seconds if something was not right. "Did you all have fun last night with the Watkins'? Where did you have dinner?"

Her parents both nodded their heads and her mother offered, "They hosted us at their yacht club. It was seafood night and the stone crabs were fresh and delicious."

Her father interrupted her mother. "Jennifer, you know we have always been direct with you." He continued on. "Your mother and I are not thrilled with your latest boyfriend."

Jennifer started to speak, but her father said, "Let me finish. Of course, we only met him for a few minutes, but you understand, with age comes wisdom. There was something about him that didn't sit well with your mother and me. It's not anything you can put your finger on. He just appeared too smooth and not as sincere as he'd probably like to come across. Jennifer, you know that we love you and have always wanted the best for you and can't tell you what to do. But please, darling, don't fall for the outside charm. There is something with this fellow that just doesn't sit right with us."

Jennifer's heart sank after hearing this reaction about Javier from her parents. "Dad, maybe it's just his Spanish culture that's throwing you off. I do have to admit that he exudes charm, but I was formally introduced to him by a lady who has known his family for years. She can't say enough nice things about him and his upbringing. Maybe over time, you'll change your minds. All I can tell you is that he has been extremely sweet and considerate to me and I really like him."

"Jennifer, again, we can't tell you what to do. For all we know, your Javier could be a saint. But honestly, we don't get the impression. All we can ask is that you be aware and keep your guard up. Are you seeing him again today?"

"Yes Dad, we're going to play a little tennis and maybe go for a bike ride." After hearing her parents' opinion of Javier, she didn't want to elaborate on her plans. She knew from past experience, that no guy was good enough for their little girl. Plus, she figured that his Spanish suavity turned them off. She knew that the "kiss of death" occurred when Javier had kissed her mother's hand last night. Needless to say, she was unhappy with their conversation. But she appreciated their input to an extent and would store it in the back of her mind. She grabbed a glass of orange juice.

"Jennifer, aren't you joining us for breakfast?" her mother asked.

"No, Mom, I have to take a shower and get dressed for the day." As she walked out of the room, she stopped and gave each of them a kiss. She felt perturbed that her parents weren't crazy about Javier. Their comments cast a slight shadow of doubt over her.

Javier rang the bell at 10:00 on the dot. When she opened the door and saw him dressed in his tennis whites with a yellow cashmere sweater nonchalantly tied around his shoulders, her parents' earlier comments became a distant memory. She thought twice about inviting him into the house, but noticed that her parents had finished breakfast and were doing their own things around the house. Javier immediately embraced her. She knew that she looked especially good in her white Bolle tennis dress, trimmed with pink ribbon. She too was wearing a pink cashmere sweater around her neck. She asked Javier to wait in the living room while she got her straw visor and racket bag. She looked at him and said, "Are you ready to get crushed on the tennis court?"

He replied, "I'm ready to get crushed by you anywhere , just not on a tennis court." They headed out the door. The Porsche was parked with the top down. After they got in, Jennifer gave Javier directions to the club, which was only a few minutes away from her house.

When they arrived, she checked in at the tennis center and located the clay court that had been reserved for them. They played for about an hour and a half. Jennifer was initially distracted by Javier's tanned athletic body, and couldn't get her rhythm, but was determined to let her skills outshine her opponent, even if he were gorgeous. She had to admit that he put up a good fight. They were pretty evenly matched but she prevailed. Out of the three close sets they played, he won one while she beat him in the other two. After acing her serve in the final game of the last set, Javier came over to the net, bowing down to her and saying, "I can't take anymore of this punishment. My darling, you are too good. I adore the way you look when you are ready to kill the ball." Then he kissed her.

Even though he was perspiring, Jennifer was still attracted to his scent. "Javier, I promise, no more punishment, let's have lunch." They ambled over to the clubhouse arm in arm.

After a light lunch, Jennifer suggested they rent bikes in the Grove and she would take him on a tour of the neighborhood. They had a lovely ride down Main Highway and then onto Old Cutler Road. They stopped at a park to take a break. Sitting on a bench under an old banyan tree, they kissed and hugged each other. Jennifer could feel Javier fondling her breasts. She could sense that her nipples were hard from the sensation of his touch. "Mi amor," he said, "I want all of you. I want to taste every part of your body. Please, my love, you are killing me. I have such a desire for all of you."

Jennifer looked at this remarkable man and said, "Javier, remember next week I'm coming up for the ball. Depending on how sweet you are to me and of course, how much you beg your wish just might get fulfilled."

"Mi amor, you are such a tease." He continued kissing her. She was getting hotter by the second but knew they had to head back. It was already 5:00 and she didn't want them to get stuck on their bikes in the dark. Reluctantly, they both climbed back onto their bikes. While riding back to the bike store, Jennifer could feel the sensitivity of the seat rubbing between her legs. She fantasized about how wonderful it would feel to have Javier's penis rubbing between her legs.

Before Jennifer knew it, she was waving goodbye to Javier. They'd had had a delightful weekend together. She was so relieved that he had figured out a way to work around Tate Yardley. Jennifer was looking forward to doing business together. She knew that he could give her the boost she needed to be a star broker. She couldn't wait until next weekend for the ball. Javier had told her that there would be many influential and wealthy guests sitting at their table that he was looking forward to introducing her to. She recalled him saying to her, "Jennifer, on the island, the balls raise a lot of funds for the charities, but the goal of the majority of the guests attending is to generate business opportunities. Together, with your beauty and my reputation in the world of finance, I look forward to opening many doors for us both."

Chapter 25

During the week, Jennifer heard from Javier several times a day. On Wednesday when he phoned he told her that he had established another company, JCI, solely to be used as a trading account at Tate Yardley. He told her that he would sign any necessary new account papers and would provide the firm with his corporate resolution papers. After she opened the account, he would make a "good faith" five million-dollar deposit and direct his hedge fund trading through this account with her. Jennifer couldn't have been more thrilled. Despite her parents' sentiments about Javier, he was certainly turning out to be a man of his word.

On Thursday, after the account had been opened and the deposit cleared, Lowell's squirrelly body made its way to Jennifer's desk. She knew that there was no way on earth that this guy would ever pay her a compliment, but he did say, "Jennifer, as of today, you've achieved the asset goal I had set for you. Now it's up to you to generate the commissions. I don't have to repeat our office target to you. All I can say is that your life around here will be a lot easier if you pump up your commissions." Despite his back-handed compliment, Jennifer was confident that her affiliation with Javier would make Lowell's head-spin.

Javier called on Friday morning to confirm the logistics of the trading that would occur in the JCI account. He told her that his right hand man, Serge, would probably be calling her with trading instructions. He suggested that she mark all the trades "unsolicited," and just take the orders, get them executed and DTC the shares purchased back to JCI on settlement. Jennifer noticed that Javier's voice got very serious when he switched over to business. It was weird for her to hear him that way. But she knew that they would be dealing with lots of money and he was a very responsible person. Since she really was a neophyte in the business she was hoping that she wouldn't screw anything up. After all, he was trying to help her launch a successful career and she would make it a point never to disappoint him.

"My darling Jennifer..." His voice suddenly reverted to the Javier she knew. "Tomorrow we will be together. How about coming up earlier in the day, so we can play?"

Jennifer thought that scenario out quickly. She wanted to see him earlier, but she also wanted to have the luxury of getting ready in her own room, where she could take the time to prepare at her own pace and in her own surroundings. She felt that since she was staying over anyway, a couple of extra hours wouldn't make a big difference. "Javier, I can't wait to see you also. But, you know, I really want to take the time to look extra special for you."

"My darling, you couldn't possibly look more beautiful than you are. But I understand, so I'll have the car come for you around 6:00. You'll probably be up here at 7:00, and we will have a chance to talk before going to Mar a Lago at 8:00. How is that?"

"Javier, it sounds like a perfect plan."

"Oh, Jennifer, by the way, I tried to reserve the suite for you at the Brazilian Court, but unfortunately it's sold out due to the out-of-towners attending the ball. My house has so many bedrooms. How about you pick out the one you like best?"

Jennifer smiled to herself. She knew there was more than one hotel on the island, but she also knew Javier's ultimate plan for the evening. "Javier, I'm sure I will. Who knows, Saturday may be your lucky night!"

"Mi amor, don't tease me like that on the phone. You're not even here and my body is reacting to you. Let's leave this discussion until tomorrow. I can't wait to kiss you. Have a good evening and I'll see you then."

Jennifer never asked, but was wondering what he was doing tonight? Now that she really liked him, she didn't want to share Javier. But the fact of the matter was that whatever his plans were for this evening, he was taking her to the ball tomorrow and it appeared that all his attention was focused on her. There was no point in thinking about all that now. She had a mani/pedi appointment in half an hour and had made plans with her parents to join them for dinner at the club at 7:30. She was looking forward to telling them how she was forging ahead in her business and also inform them about her plans for the rest of the weekend.

At 7:45, Jennifer and her parents were sitting down to dinner at the country club. They had just given the waiter their requests for dinner and her father was taking a sip of his scotch and soda. Due to conflicting schedules, they hadn't sat down to dinner as a family in nearly a week. While her dad was enjoying his drink, her mother asked how things at work were going. Jennifer told them about how Lowell had come to her this past week and basically let her know that she had job security for the foreseeable future based on her asset gathering success. She mentioned how competitive and cut-throat she found the business to be. She relayed to them the greed of the firm and the brokers and about how the needs of the clients were totally ignored for the sake of generating higher revenues. She told her dad that the business was nothing like it used to be when she accompanied him to the brokerage firm as a little girl.

"Well Jennifer," her father said, "we tried to protect you from this." Without actually saying, "we told you so," he intimated that they were well aware of how tawdry the business had become.

"But Dad," Jennifer continued, "despite all of this, I am beginning to succeed, and have some foundations in place that will help me rise above the rest. Believe me, I have no intention of stooping to the level of a money hungry salesman looking to take advantage of their clients. I will make you proud." She knew better than to tell them about her business relationship with Javier.

After their main course was served, her father asked her if she was still seeing Javier. "Of course I am. As a matter of fact, I was going to tell you both this evening that I'm heading back up to Palm Beach tomorrow. One of my clients invited us to sit at her table for the Red Cross Ball. It's going to be at Mar-a-Lago and is supposedly 'the' event of the season. I'm really looking forward to it."

"Well honey, you know we always wish the best for you, but do keep in mind our feelings about your gentleman friend."

Hearing her father repeat his opinion regarding Javier she decided to change the subject and discuss topics relating to them. Since he had been named Chief of Staff of the hospital, her father was involved more in its day to day administrative duties. The position was considered to be quite prestigious in the medical community. She asked him how he was enjoying his new role and how he balanced out his practice with the duties at the hospital. He mentioned to Jennifer and her mother that maybe, in retrospect, it would have been better to have turned down the offer. He had no idea of the amount of politics involved. Jennifer knew that her parents abhorred gossip and in-house squabbling. She surmised that even in the field of medicine there were challenges to be dealt with.

Her mother discussed the plans she was making as chairman of the American Heart Association. Her new project was to raise funds to bring heart-healthy menus back to the school system. Her primary focus was on the elementary schools. "We are trying to instill healthy eating habits in the young. I'm sure you've read the studies reporting that obesity and diabetes are becoming a national epidemic. And the only way to beat it is to teach children healthy eating habits at an early age. Jennifer, maybe down the road you can ask your firm to sponsor an event for us. It would be great PR for them and maybe attract some new clients for you."

They all passed on dessert, especially after just discussing the topics of obesity and diabetes.

By the time they drove back to the house it was 10:30. Jennifer was happy that she could get to bed early and have a good night's sleep. As she laid her head on the pillow she thought of tomorrow evening. She imagined herself on Javier's arm, majestically walking into the main ballroom of Mar-a-Lago. And just before falling into a deep slumber, she fantasized of feeling Javier's body next to hers in bed. Just the thought of making passionate love to him all night long sent a chill through her body, only to be followed by the warmth of desire.

Chapter 26

Saturday flew by. Before she knew it, Jennifer was packing her bags for the next day and a half. The very first item she grabbed was her pink Natori nightgown. She had never worn it before and thought that tonight it would make its debut. Since she didn't know what Javier's plans were for tomorrow, she selected a white Capri ensemble and Panama hat as well as a warm-up suit with sneakers. That way she was prepared for an elegant Sunday brunch or a run along the beach. After a hot steam and shower she sat down at her vanity. While gazing at her reflection in the mirror she noticed how naturally flushed her cheeks were. The anticipation of being with Javier caused a natural rush through her body. Actually, she thought, the exhilaration she had been feeling for the last couple of weeks was reminiscent of the high that one experiences at the onset of a new and exciting relationship. Her mother, though, had taught her over the years to cherish that joyous emotion, because as time passes, the heightened attraction slowly fades into a smoldering love and then to an everlasting unbreakable bond of friendship. That is, only if you selected the "right" person with whom you share a mutual love and respect. Jennifer was hopeful that Javier was the "right" man for her.

After meticulously applying her make-up, Jennifer put on her Valentino gown. As she draped it over her body, she could feel the softness of the silk jersey caress her skin. She was definitely in a heightened mental and physical state.

Promptly at 6:00 the doorbell rang. Jennifer took one more look at her image in the full-length mirror. The red dress against her flawless skin and flowing, shiny blond hair was quite striking. She couldn't wait to see Javier's reaction.

Before walking out the door, she went into the study where her parents were both reading to bid them goodbye. Her father looked up. "Jennifer, you look beautiful."

Her mother had tears in her eyes. "My little girl, how magnificent you are!"

Her parents weren't usually so vocal with their compliments, so Jennifer knew that she must really look great. She gave each of them a kiss and said, "I'll be home late tomorrow afternoon. And, please don't worry about me. I'm in good hands."

Her father gave her a look and said, "If you say so but frankly I'm not so convinced. Whatever the case, Jennifer, be safe and have a good time."

Her mother walked her to the door, helping her with the garment bag and valise. At the entrance, the driver took the luggage and packed it away in the car's trunk. As Jennifer sat down in the back seat, this time, she found a red rose next to a sealed envelope. She opened and read the single sentence, "My darling, I can't wait to taste you." As the car pulled out of the motor court, Jennifer felt the heat rising in her body.

Within an hour, the tires of the Town Car were rolling onto the gravel driveway in front of Javier's home. All the lights in the house were on. As the car made its way to the port couchere, she saw Javier in his tuxedo awaiting her arrival. The inner excitement within her was mounting. She couldn't wait to get out of the car to hug him. Javier seemed equally excited to see Jennifer. As soon as the car came to a halt, he opened her door. After he helped her out, he took a step backward. "Bellissima, you are gorgeous. How is it that every time we meet, you look more beautiful?" He took her in his arms and gave her a kiss that made her melt in his arms. While they were embracing, the driver took her valises into the house. Jennifer was thrilled that Javier had reacted so strongly to her. She could have made love to him right then and there. He was handsome in his tuxedo with pleated silk shirt and white tie. She noticed that instead of the typical black patent shoes, he was wearing Ferragamo slip-ons without socks. It was very au currant. Jennifer loved his look and his scent was equally intoxicating. They walked into the house arm in arm. Javier offered her a drink. She opted for a glass of Pellegrino since she wanted to be lucid for the ball. Jennifer wanted to experience all the evening had to offer. Javier had a Dewar's on the rocks. "Mi amor, you look beautiful, let's sit down for a minute and discuss our strategy." He led them to a couch in the living room.

Jennifer was a little confused. "What do you mean when you say our strategy?"

"Mi amor, as I mentioned last weekend when we were together on that lovely bike ride, that this ball is a grand social occasion, but my darling, it will also give us a chance to meet potential new clients and help launch your career. Mercedes has been kind enough to arrange for us to be seated with the titans of business. Just at our table alone, will be the chairman of the largest international beverage company as well the CFO of a music distribution company. She told me that she also invited a Russian oligarch who is the vodka producer to the world. My darling, we are going on a safari tonight, but only hunting for elephants. Between your beauty and me by your side, we will lasso them in."

Jennifer was caught a little off guard by the fact that there was a planned strategy for the evening. She had been looking forward to just having a good time. But, she reasoned, Javier was right, this was an opportunity to help put her career on the fast track. There was no way she would ever have access to these types of people. They weren't the "one -percenters," they were in the one tenth of one percent earners. She was glad that Javier had had this discussion with her.

"But Javier, I didn't even bring my business cards. It didn't even occur to me carry them to a social affair."

"No problems my darling, Mercedes will insure that all interested parties have your contact information." Javier stood up and held out his hand to assist Jennifer. "Let's make a toast to a fun and successful evening." They each sipped their drink and then he gave Jennifer a long, tender kiss on her lips.

Chapter 27

For the evening, Javier had decided to drive his white Bentley coupe. "Darling, I thought you would be more comfortable in the Bentley tonight. We wouldn't want to crush your beautiful gown." Jennifer couldn't believe that he owned so many cars. They definitely shared many of the same passions.

Mar-A-Lago was a short drive from El Vedado Way, south on AIA. As they drove up, the main building was bathed in a sea of pink lighting. Their car was in a queue heading toward the main entrance where a battalion of uniformed valets was parking the cars. In the line was every type of exotic car one could imagine, from Ferraris and Lamborghinis to a few Rolls Royce Phantoms, as well as long white limousines. Women getting out of the cars looked resplendent in their couture gowns. Jennifer was happy that she had decided to splurge on her Valentino after all. When their car came up to the entrance, one of the valets opened Jennifer's door and assisted her out. Javier came around to get her offering her his arm as they walked in. Cocktails were being served by the pool area. A four-piece band was playing light contemporary music. There must have been hundreds of guests there. "Darling, what may I get you to drink?"

"Thank you, Javier, just a glass of Sauvignon Blanc, please."

"I'll be right back, don't leave this spot. I don't want to lose you."

A waiter came up to Jennifer and held out a silver serving platter of baby lamb chops. Jennifer loved lamb chops, but tonight didn't want to risk getting anything on her dress. She stood there admiring the scene of beautiful people. All the fashion designers were duly represented. Jennifer saw gowns by Yves St Laurent, Dior, Chanel and even a Valentino very similar to hers but with a much lower neckline. The jewelry was beyond belief. Necklaces and earrings were just dripping in diamonds. Jennifer even noticed that quite a few of the ladies were wearing diamond tiaras in their hair. The weather was perfectly clear and a full moon reflected on the swimming pool and the fountains in the courtyard. By the time Javier returned, Jennifer had absorbed her surroundings. Before they took a sip of their drinks, Javier held up his glass and said, "To the most gorgeous woman at the ball and to our successful safari." The cold dry wine tasted good in Jennifer's mouth. She really felt happy to be here with Javier.

All of a sudden, out of nowhere, Mercedes came up behind Javier, extending both arms around his waist. He turned to see it was her. "Mercedes, you look beautiful." He gave her a hug and a kiss on the lips.

"My darlings, I am so glad you are here with me. This is one of my favorite charity balls and I just know that you both will have a grand time." Taking Javier's arm, she continued, saying, "Come with me, I'd like to introduce you to my other guests." The three of them walked over to the other side of the courtyard approaching a seating area where several couples were talking together. "Everyone, I'd like you to meet my special friends, this is Jennifer Palmer, my brand new gorgeous stockbroker and Javier Cordova, one of the smartest and handsomest men on the island."

They all introduced themselves to one another and made room for Jennifer and Javier to sit down. Jennifer saw how Javier immediately plunged into conversation with the group. He seemed to perk everybody up with his lively repartee. Just as they were all warming up to each other, the band stopped playing and the dinner bell was rung. Jennifer took Javier's arm and joined the exquisitely dressed guests making their way into the ballroom. Mercedes was walking right behind them. "Our tables are number two and three, right by the dance floor."

The room was drop-dead gorgeous. Even though it was a Red Cross Ball, everything was in white. Lit candles created a soft glow. The centerpieces were three-foot high arrangements of white roses with calla lilies. The tables had white satin and silver tablecloths. Each guest dining chair was wrapped in white satin with a big bow tied in the back. A ten-piece orchestra was on the stage playing classical music as the group walked in. Mercedes led them to her tables. Everyone waited for her to direct them to their appointed seats. "Ok my friends," she said. "Just to make things a little more interesting, I'm going to split everyone up. That way, you'll each have a chance to meet two new friends."

Jennifer was seated at table #3 and Javier was at table #2 with Mercedes. Each table sat 10 guests. Before taking his seat, Javier helped Jennifer into hers, whispering in her ear, "Mi amor, I will miss you, but remember, we are on safari." He gave her a kiss on the cheek and went over to his table.

After sitting down, everyone went around the table introducing themselves. The waiters poured wine into the crystal goblets. Jennifer found herself seated next to George Malone on her left and Dimitri Stravinsko on her right. George was a distinguished looking older gentleman with thick silver hair. Jennifer thought that he bore an uncanny resemblance to the actor, John Forsythe. Dimitri was quite heavy set. He had a beard and a thick accent. Over his tuxedo shirt, was a gold chain with a large medallion hanging from it. Even though it appeared odd for a man to wear such ornate jewelry, Dimitri could carry it off. Jennifer asked him where he was from and he replied, "I am Russian, from St. Petersburg. Have you ever been to my country?" Jennifer assumed that this was the Russian oligarch Javier had mentioned to her earlier.

"Yes Dimitri, I actually visited St. Petersburg as well as Moscow."

"How did you like my country?"

"Well honestly, I was there twice with my parents. The first time was when the country was under Communist rule and then later after it became a Democratic society."

"And Jennifer, did you notice any changes?"

"Your country appeared to be in better physical shape under Communism. The second time we were there it appeared as though the infrastructure was in a state of neglect. The roads were a mess, potholes everywhere. The buildings in the cities, especially St. Petersburg looked as though they were falling apart. Even the Hermitage had lots of broken windows and appeared to be in a state of disrepair. Our tour guide had told us that her life was worse off than before. She had an engineering degree, but had to work as a guide since there were no jobs available in her industry. She also mentioned that the country was being run by the Russian mafia. And in order to get anything done, you had to bribe the city officials."

Jennifer could tell that Dimitri looked annoyed when she mentioned the Russian mafia, so she thought it best to change the subject. "Dimitri, do you live in the States now and how did you learn to speak English so well?"

"Jennifer, I am only here for my business. The U.S. is a big consumer of my product, so I travel here once or twice a year. When I was a teenager, my parents sent me to school in England, where I learned to speak English. Right now my main residence is still in Russia, since that is where my company is based. But I spend all summer in the South of France on my yacht."

"What type of product do you make?"

Dimitri smiled and said proudly, "My dear, my company is the largest producer of Russian vodka. We sell our product to almost every country in the world. But as I told you before, your country is our biggest consumer."

Jennifer was impressed and felt fortunate that Mercedes had sat her next to Dimitri. As they continued to chat, the first course of caviar with blinis was served.

"Now I feel at home, with my Russian caviar. All I need is a shot of vodka." Dimitri looked around for the waiter who quickly appeared to take his drink request.

While Dimitri was talking to the waiter, Jennifer turned to speak with her other tablemate, George. She sensed that he was definitely a lower key person than Dimitri. She asked him if he was from the South Florida area. He told her that they have a home in Palm Beach where they stay through the winter months but his main residence is in Chicago. "Are you originally from Illinois?" she asked.

"I'm a born and bred Chicagoan. My family has lived there through several generations. We love the city; it's just the winters that drive us down here. Jennifer, Mercedes mentioned that you were her stockbroker. Not only are you pretty but smart. What firm are you with?"

Jennifer was pleased that George had picked up on the fact that she was a broker. "I'm with Tate Yardley."

"Know the firm well. They have an office just blocks away from our corporate headquarters on Wacker Street. How long have you been with them?"

Jennifer didn't want to lie, but she also wasn't keen on admitting that she had been in the business for less than a year. "Well actually, George, I have been investing in the stock market since I was thirteen."

"So Jennifer, you must be a seasoned investor by now. What are your thoughts on the current global economic crisis and its effects on the markets?"

Jennifer had not been prepared for such intense questioning, but still managed to reply with a solid answer that seemed to satisfy George. She then decided to turn the tables and ask George about what business he was involved in.

"We are in the soft drink business."

"What role do you have in the company?"

"My grandfather founded the company way back in the thirties, during the Great Depression. And then my father took over the reins and in turn, after his passing, I became Chairman of the Board."

As George was speaking, Jennifer was thinking about how right Javier had been about going "on safari" tonight. There was no way in the world that she would ever come into contact with the men sitting on either side of her. She would do her best to take full advantage of this wonderful opportunity without of course, appearing overly aggressive. The salad had been served but she was too involved with her discussion with George to take a bite. While an intermezzo was served before the main course, Javier came over and asked her to dance. She couldn't wait to tell him about her dining companions. Once on the dance floor, he took her in his arms and put his mouth up to her ear. "My darling, how are you enjoying yourself?"

"Javier, you were right, I'm sitting between two dynamic businessmen. We appear to be getting along quite well. I can't believe Mercedes sat me at this great table."

"Darling, Mercedes knows more than you can imagine. Like me, she really wants to help you. I' m so glad you are having a good time. Make sure though, that before the evening is finished, they commit to seeing you again. The key to getting the big elephants is to lasso them in slowly."

They continued to dance and Jennifer saw how many people were watching them on the dance floor. She knew that they made a striking couple. Just as the song was ending, Dimitri came over to them and asked if Jennifer would like to dance with him. She looked at Javier and he gave her a knowing wink. "Of course, Dimitri, it would be my honor to dance with you."

While they were dancing together, Dimitri told her that she was the most beautiful woman in the room. "The young man with you, is he your husband or lover?"

Jennifer blushed. "No, Dimitri, he's my boyfriend."

"Jennifer, you can tell me, is he just one of many boyfriends?"

"No, Dimitri, right now he's the one and only."

"A beautiful swan like you should always have many men to choose from. Never settle for just one. No matter, you must promise me that you will come to the South of France next summer; no, let's make it earlier, in the spring. I will send one of my jets to pick you up and then you will stay on the yacht. I assure you that you will have the time of your life."

Jennifer smiled at him and was ready to head back to the table when the song had ended. Dimitri held on to her hand, saying, "Jennifer, I didn't hear your answer..."

Jennifer thought to herself, if that is what it took to get him as a client, why not say yes? Plus, a lot could happen between now and then. "Yes, Dimitri, I will come."

He walked her back to the table and pulled out her chair to sit down. The main course was just being served. All the plates had large silver oval covers to keep the food warm. After the plates were delivered to each guest, the silver warmers were dramatically taken off in unison to reveal the main event, beef tenderloin accompanied with roasted potatoes, a broccoli puree and miniature vegetables. The waiters came by, refilling half-empty wine glasses. As the guests leisurely consumed their main course, the band played dinner music.

While Jennifer had been dancing with Javier, George and Dimitri had struck up a friendship. During dinner the three of them chatted a little about politics and general world events. They all agreed that the climate for international business was undergoing some of the biggest challenges ever faced in generations and it appeared as though the current economic crisis was far from any kind of resolution.

As the guests finished their main course, the waiters began to clear the tables in preparation for dessert. The band struck up with dance music and Javier came back to dance with Jennifer. While dancing to "The Best is Yet to Come," Javier held Jennifer in his arms. Their bodies swayed together to the rhythm. "Bellissima," he said, "I am making very good contacts at my table as well. There is a widow on my right who inherited her husband's fortune and on my left is a divorcee who runs a multi-national advertising company. They admired you from a distance and asked me what you did. I told them that you handled investments for Tate Yardley. They are both keenly interested in meeting you. After this dance, I will take you over and introduce you to the ladies."

"Javier, I wish this evening would never end. I can't believe the amount of wealth that is represented here." The song ended and Javier gave her a kiss before leading her over to his table. The two elegant ladies looked up at her. Javier said, "Delores and Jeanette, I'd like you to meet Jennifer Palmer. Jennifer, why don't you sit in my chair and chat with the ladies while I ask our hostess to dance."

Jennifer sat down with the two ladies. They were both peppering her with questions about herself and seemed to be quite interested in her responses. During their conversation, Jennifer noticed Javier dancing with Mercedes. Just like at Taboo two weeks ago, they were dancing like lovers do. But Jennifer knew better, even though it did appear a bit odd to her, they were just good friends that enjoyed each other's company. Plus, the Latin men always made a woman feel extra special. Jennifer was just grateful that Mercedes had included her in this beautiful event. Jennifer brought her mind back to the conversation with Delores and Jeanette. Apparently they were both friends and based on their previous conversation with Javier, wanted to pursue Jennifer. They proposed meeting her for lunch in Palm Beach during the upcoming week. Jennifer was ecstatic at her reception from this collection of erudite people.

Before she knew it, Javier was walking back to the table with Mercedes. "Ladies, I'm sure you had an engaging conversation with the beautiful Jennifer. I told you she was a smart lady." Javier held out his arm to escort her back to her table. He whispered in her ear, "What a combination we have created: love and business."

Waiting at her seat was a red velvet cupcake and petit fours along with George and Dimitri. Apparently she had cast her spell of charm on the two.

The evening was beginning to wind down. The orchestra was playing "Last Dance" and guests were slowly drifting out of the ballroom. Both George and Dimitri gave Jennifer a kiss good-bye. With a twinkle in his eye, Dimitri held both of Jennifer's hands and said, "I look forward to hosting you on my yacht this spring. Don't disappoint me."

Jennifer headed over to Javier's table, which had been vacated except for Mercedes and Javier, who were in deep conversation. When she quietly sat down next to him, they halted their discussion. Mercedes immediately spoke out, "Jennifer, you looked beautiful this evening; I sincerely hope you had a good time and I want you to know how enamored my friends were with you. I will make sure they have all your numbers. It seems as though Delores and Jeanette are looking forward to meeting you next week, they are lovely ladies and besides that, they are loaded."

"Mercedes, I can't thank you enough. The evening was magnificent and I look forward to assisting your friends with their investments. You are a real friend."

They all walked out of the ballroom to the valet stand. Mercedes' car and driver was waiting for her. Before she got in, they kissed and bid each other good-bye. Javier's Bentley was brought up to the entrance. As he settled into the driver's seat, the valet helped Jennifer in to the passenger seat. Javier steered the car out of the club's massive gates, heading back to El Vedado Way. He had his hand on Jennifer's thigh throughout the trip back to the house. She could feel his heat through her gown. Jennifer was excited about all the evening's happenings, but was trembling with excitement about what was yet to come.

After parking the car by the front door, Javier leaned over and gave Jennifer a long seductive kiss. "My darling, we were separated for much too long this evening. I have missed you beyond belief. Let's head inside."

Once inside the house, he gave her a French kiss, gently slipping his hand inside the top of her gown and fondling her breasts. Jennifer could sense the excitement in her body. Her nipples were sensitive and hard. He leaned over and picked her up, carrying her into his bedroom. Her arms were around his neck and she was kissing his face. He smelled so good. She adored his lips and the taste of his mouth. She had longed for this moment of passion. Slowly he pulled off her gown, letting it fall to the foot of the bed. He laid her down, kicking off his shoes and releasing his tie. He fell on the bed beside her. They rolled around embracing and kissing each other. He grabbed her breasts and sank his face into them. Without saying a word he slipped off her panties and took off his trousers. She felt his hardness penetrate her core. They made love until dawn and passed out from sheer exhaustion, entering a deep sleep.

Jennifer woke up first, looking at the clock and seeing that it was already noon. Javier still had his arms around her. She looked up at his handsome face. As if feeling her gaze, he opened up his eyes, smiling and bringing her even closer to him. "My darling angel, last night was heavenly. I adore every part of you." They passionately locked their lips again, clinging even tighter to each other.

"Bellissima, I am starving. Since we obviously slept through breakfast, let's have lunch by the pool. I'll arrange for my housekeeper to assemble a feast for us. Why don't you take a shower and we'll meet on the terrace." Jennifer watched as his nude body got out of bed. It was tanned and taut. After he walked out of the room, she got up and made a beeline to the shower. She first looked in the mirror to assess the damage from last night. Her make-up had held up pretty well, no smears or streaks. She couldn't wait to take a long, hot shower. As she got out, she noticed that Javier had left a white, fluffy, terrycloth robe for her, emblazoned with his initials.

After drying herself off and brushing her hair out, she made her way to the terrace overlooking the pool and Lake Worth. It was a magnificent day. Cool and crisp with not a cloud in the sky. She found Javier waiting for her, reading the *New York Times* business section. The table was set up with a white tablecloth and a vase of hydrangeas. They each had a big bowl of spinach salad topped with a scoop each of chopped egg and chicken salad. Jennifer didn't realize how hungry she really was. They both dug in and devoured their salads barely exchanging a word. When they were finished the housekeeper came back out with a platter of just-baked chocolate chip cookies. She cleared the table and asked if they wanted anything else. Contentedly, they nibbled on their cookies. Jennifer was so happy that she couldn't stop smiling at Javier. She was still basking in the warmth of the previous night's lovemaking. Javier was caressing her arm. "Mi amor, you were the belle of the ball last night. Everyone loved you and Mercedes will be contacting them to arrange to get together with you. My darling, please excuse me for discussing business. You don't mind? No?"

"It's fine, Javier, go ahead."

"Well once they do connect with you, it is important that you arrange for a meeting as soon as possible. There is that American saying, 'Strike while the fire is hot.' Since all these prospective clients have amassed large fortunes, you would be overwhelmed with actively managing it all. So the best transition is for you to suggest that they place their funds with Cordova Investments. You could mention to them that Tate Yardley always puts their client's interests first and Cordova Investments is your firm's number one recommendation for them. You will get all the necessary information we need to open the accounts as well as a check made out to Cordova Investments. Once the accounts are opened with us and the checks have cleared, I will direct all trading activity to you through the account we opened at Tate Yardley last week."

Quite suddenly, the warmth that carried over from last night began to feel like the chill of a cold shower. What in the hell was Javier talking about?

"Javier, I don't understand your point. I thought that all this time, you were encouraging these people to do business with me. Don't you recall that I told you that Tate Yardley does not want to be associated with your firm, under any circumstances? And now you want me to jeopardize my career? I really don't get it."

"Mi amor, you don't understand."

"Mi amor to you, frankly I don't. Was this your plan all along? And then to top it off, you seduce me." Jennifer was enraged. It was hard for her to comprehend the fact that they had just spent the night making love and a few hours later, in the light of day, he's discussing this bizarre business proposition.

In a pleading tone he said, "Bellissima, please hear me out. I'm doing this solely to help you. Because of me, you will have so much trading activity that you will become the shining star of your office if not the entire firm. Don't look so sad. You have to understand that there is no way, with your limited experience, that you could start managing hundreds of millions of dollars. I will take that liability and responsibility off your shoulders and simply send the trades your way. Don't you see everyone wins? The clients will have one of the best money managers in the country and you will be financially rewarded. I love you my darling, please don't over-analyze this. Believe me; down the road you will be grateful. Now, mi amor let me see that beautiful smile of yours."

Jennifer started to think that maybe Javier was right after all. She did know in her heart that she didn't have the tools to manage that size of assets. And she was comfortable with the fact that the funds would be safe with him. *Forbes* doesn't just name anyone "Money Manager of the Year." And as he said, she still would be making a tremendous sum of money, without the liability. The only little nudge was telling investors that Tate Yardley worked with Cordova Investments. She knew that she could deal with that since she wasn't doing anything wrong or illegal, just the right thing for high net worth individuals. In retrospect, it sounded like a good plan.

Javier stood up and walked over to her, holding her face in his hands, "I'm waiting for the Jennifer smile."

She stood up and they embraced. "Javier, I'm sorry. I didn't mean to doubt you or your intentions. Thank you for looking after my best interests. I truly appreciate it."

While they continued to hug, she felt Javier's right hand move off her back. It seemed as though he were reaching for something in his pocket. "My darling, I have a special gift for you." He presented her with a red Cartier box. She was totally taken aback. "Here, let me open it for you." As she lifted up the top of the box, she saw a gold Love Bracelet. She had long admired this piece. "If I may, I'd like to put this on your wrist?"

She held out her hand and with a small gold screwdriver that came with the bracelet, he placed it on her wrist and tightened the screws at each end. Nonchalantly, he slipped the gold screwdriver into his pocket. She held her wrist out admiring the shiny bracelet as it sparkled in the sunshine. Hugging him close to her, she knew that this was a special man who sincerely cared for her. What a beautiful ending to a glorious weekend.

Jennifer wore her jogging outfit on the ride home. With the convertible top of the Porsche down, it protected her from the chill as they sped south on the turnpike. Javier held her hand during the drive down to Miami. Once parked at her house, he carried her valises to the front door. "Would you like to come in?" Jennifer asked.

"No, my darling, it's Sunday night. I'd like to get back early so I can decompress myself for the upcoming week." He leaned down and gave her a tender French kiss. As he walked back to his car, he turned around and said, "Don't be surprised if my trader gives you a call before the opening bell tomorrow. I promise, I won't let you down." He got in his car and made a quick U-turn heading back home to Palm Beach.

Chapter 28

Jennifer had retired early the previous evening. She had been emotionally and physically exhausted from all of the weekend's activities, but had woken up fresh and ready to take on the day. She was at her desk bright and early. While reading the day's market research, her phone rang. She couldn't imagine who would be calling her at 8:00 in the morning. Her caller ID read: name unavailable. She decided to answer it anyway. The voice on the other end began, "Jennifer Palmer, I'm an associate of Javier Cordova's, my name is Oscar. He has asked me to call you and give you a market order for 100,000 shares of Northern Ocean Works, the symbol NOW at the opening. He said you know the account it will be purchased in. Also, please make sure it's DVP'd from his account on settlement. Please confirm these instructions." She read the order back to him. "Thank you, Jennifer. We will speak again soon."

As soon as they hung up, she checked the previous closing price of the stock. She saw that last Friday, it had finished the day at $43 per share. So far, this morning's opening offer was $43.30. Without doing the math, Jennifer realized that this transaction would amount to over $4,000,000. By then, it was 8:40 a.m. She noticed that due to good news in the overseas markets, the S & P Futures were up big, implying a strong opening. Jennifer felt that it would be smart to get the order queued up in the system as soon as possible. After pulling up the account which Javier had opened with her last week, she placed the order for 100,000 shares of NOW. At the last checkpoint before submitting the order the totals appeared specifying the amount that would be debited from the account. It was on this screen that Jennifer saw that her commission for placing the trade would be $35,000. She incredulously reviewed the numbers again. In the last six months since she had started at Tate Yardley, she had earned slightly more than that amount. Now, in just one trade, she would generate that revenue. Even though Tate Yardley earned 65% of the total transaction cost, she would still get 35%, plus her gross commissions would reflect the total amount. Net-net insuring her job security. She wondered if she would hear from Lowell during the day after he saw the trade hit. At this point, she really didn't care.

At 9:20, she received a call from a compliance officer, confirming that she had actually received an unsolicited request to place the order. The firm had a thorough system of checks and balances that were immediately launched once an order was detected that was inconsistent with a broker's previous trading patterns. If by chance, there had been a mistake of some sort, Jennifer would ultimately be financially responsible for the error. Even though the compliance department was typically looking to protect the firm, this time she was pleased that they had re-confirmed the activity with her. At 9:30, Jennifer watched as NOW traded 100,000 shares at $43.279 on the opening bell. A yellow window popped up on her screen confirming that the trade had been executed along with the net price and commissions.

When Jennifer's officemate George came in, she couldn't wait to tell him about her big trade. "Jennifer, I knew you had it in you. I'm proud of you, just be careful." George was always so conservative and practical, but why would he think that she needed to be careful?

While Jennifer was still reveling in the morning's excitement, she received a call from Javier. "I see that you filled our order for 100,000 NOW. Congratulations my darling, this is just a small taste of what is yet to come. Mercedes phoned me earlier, and told me that she had spoken with George, the gentleman sitting at your table as well as with Delores and Jeanette. She has set up meetings with the three of them with you for this week. She will phone you later with the details. And by the way, Dimitri was absolutely smitten by you. He wants to fly you on his private jet over to Nice to spend a few days on his yacht. My darling, I highly recommend you go. He told Mercedes that he has $200,000,000 that he would like to invest. Not bad for an evening's work? I love you my darling, will speak with you later."

Before Jennifer could even utter a word, he had hung up. Things were certainly moving along a lot faster than she had ever expected. Even Lowell dropped by the office after lunch to laud her on the trade.

"Jennifer, it looks like you've turned the corner. Have more days like today and you just might become a successful broker."

Jennifer just stared at him as he walked away. Lowell's 'vote of confidence' certainly didn't offer any inducement.

Over the next few weeks, Jennifer was in close touch with Mercedes who had arranged meetings for Jennifer with several of the guests that had attended the ball as well as with her clique of friends and acquaintances. A few of the appointments she had in the office, but she met with many of the prospects in Palm Beach. The more meetings she had, the easier she found it to recommend that the investors invest with Cordova Investments. By year-end she had arranged assets in excess of $50,000,000 to be managed by Javier. And as promised, Javier's trader Oscar was calling Jennifer several times a day with trading instructions. For the year, Jennifer's commissions had totaled

$500,000. This was unheard of for a new recruit to accomplish in her first year. Lowell had the year-end dinner party, which Jennifer chose not to attend. The other brokers got wind of her success and became obnoxiously jealous. She knew that she had raised the bar high and the competition would only get stiffer.

With her robust income, Jennifer was finally able to move out of her parents' house. In order to be closer to Javier, she purchased a 4,000 square foot condo in Manalapan complete with a wrap around terrace. Over the Christmas holiday, Javier had surprised her with a white Aston Martin. Jennifer couldn't be happier. She was finally living out her dream.

Chapter 29

By March, Jennifer was well on her way to becoming a member of Tate Yardley's "Chairman's Club." With transactions in her own clients' accounts as well as the business that was directed her way by Javier, her monthly commissions totaled over $100,000. Of that, her take was almost $45,000. In order to qualify, a broker had to generate in excess of $2 million gross commissions per year. The reward for attaining the goal was a trip to a yet to be determined exotic location where the firm would display all its bells and whistles to motivate the "fortunate" attendees to repeat their accomplishments the following year.

Lowell certainly had changed his tune. He was practically tripping over himself to please Jennifer. He moved her to a corner office overlooking Biscayne Bay, providing her with her own personal sales assistant. He actually came by the office every day, smiling, asking if there was anything she needed. Jennifer recalled how he had previously treated her like chopped liver, but now that the tides had changed and he was financially participating in her revenue stream, he couldn't do enough for her. She was a little surprised that he never really questioned the source of Javier's trades or the fact that the shares for each transaction on settlement were DVP'd out of the firm to an international bank. Plus, she was having conferences with prospects in the office on a daily basis, without actually opening up new accounts at Tate Yardley. She just assumed that he was grateful to participate in such a large chunk of new business that he could have cared less about the where the funds originated from. Despite this newfound success, Jennifer maintained a level head. She was well aware that the respect she was now garnering from the branch as well as the firm was as solid as her last month's production run. Everyone loves a winner, and Jennifer knew that she was in the cat's seat. More importantly to her though, was the fact their mutual clients were making money with Javier. He sent her duplicate statements so she was able to follow the progress of their accounts. Despite the crazy market volatility, he was attaining solid returns. She didn't really interact with the other brokers in the office; but could sense that they were practically pulling out whatever hair was left on their heads. She noticed that even "churn and burn" Lawrence was struggling to justify his trades.

On the weekends, Jennifer and Javier would usually be entertaining prospective clients referred by Mercedes, either at his home, the Bath and Tennis or the Everglades Club. Javier always liked to entertain in familiar surroundings. The parties became the talk of The Island. It got to the point where an invitation to their parties was the most sought over invite of the season.

The formula seemed to be working out so well, with Mercedes making the initial contacts and then once the prospects were invited to the dinner party and met their hostess, Jennifer. Many would then set up an office appointment with her during the week and then she would hand them off to Cordova Investments. It became a bit arduous to have the clients drive to Miami, so Javier arranged for his car and driver to take them down to meet with Jennifer and then back home to Palm Beach. The logistical inconvenience seemed to work to their advantage, making the arrangement that much more attractive. Once the clients met with Jennifer one on one, she succeeded in securing the necessary documents and having checks drawn directly to Cordova Investments.

Jennifer was thrilled with the success of her partnership with Javier. The only thing missing was a personal commitment. She found it to be a bit odd that they had been in an intense personal as well as sexual relationship for almost a year and only would spend time together on the weekends. She had purposely moved to Manalapan to be closer to Javier. But truth be told, he was a busy guy, managing hundreds of millions of dollars, invested globally, so he really had to be totally focused during the week. The lack of commitment really bothered her, but he certainly made it up in the quality of the time they spent together. It really would be a little self-centered of her to put any pressure on him.

During one of their quiet Sunday brunches at his house, on the pool terrace they were peacefully reading the papers and partaking of gravlax with caviar and blinis. It was a gorgeous spring day. The yachts were sailing by on Lake Worth and the mid-morning sunlight warmed up the previous evening's chill. Javier had made up a pitcher of Bloody Mary's with a kick of cayenne that they were both enjoying. The phone interrupted the quiet solitude. From Javier's side of the conversation, she gathered that it was Mercedes on the phone. "Yes, darling," Javier was saying, "I totally understand. I'm sure it won't be an issue."

Jennifer wondered what they were discussing, but feigned interest in the article she was reading. Javier seemed to be just listening, while apparently Mercedes was doing all the talking. Finally he said, "Mercedita, no worries, I'll take care of it." And hung up the phone.

"What was that all about?" Jennifer asked.

"Well, my darling your friend Dimitri called Mercedes this morning and is insisting that you fly over on his Gulfstream jet and spend a few days on his yacht docked off the shore of St Tropez."

"Javier, as you are well aware, I'm too busy to just take off a week and sashay over to the South of France. And if I go, don't you think you should come with me? Doesn't it appear a bit odd that I am flying over there alone to meet Dimitri? He knows that we have a relationship, or at least, I thought he did."

"Mi amor, I'd love to accompany you, but I think it's better for all of us if you go alone. Mercedes told me that he would invest $200 million if you went over there. Do you realize what that would mean for all of us?"

"You've got to be kidding! I knew he was wealthy, but not uber-wealthy. O.K. if you think it's worth my while and it sounds as though it is, I'll do it. Have her arrange it."

"Jennifer, since I'm sure he's not going to be handing you a check for $200 million, I need to get you our wire instructions, so all he'll need to do is sign off and we can have the funds wired directly to our bank." Javier called Mercedes back and told her that Jennifer would be happy to fly over to Europe and meet with Dimitri. While they were speaking, Jennifer was thinking that this could truly accelerate her career into the stratosphere.

Chapter 30

During the week, Mercedes had spoken with Dimitri and all the plans were finalized for Jennifer's trip. She made it a point for Mercedes to pass the message over to Dimitri that this was strictly a business trip, just to make sure that he didn't have any other ideas. She was to meet his Gulfstream V the following Friday at the Boca Raton Executive Airport. Jennifer didn't know what to pack, so she filled two valises with clothes that would fit into any possible occasion. Since she wasn't flying commercial, she knew that extra luggage wouldn't be an issue.

Jennifer spent the week getting all the loose ends resolved. Oscar had put in so many trades, that her commissions for the week had already added up to what would normally take a month to generate. Since she was no longer beholden to Lowell, she just let his onerous assistant Estelle know that she would be out of the country for about a week. She was careful though, not to mention that it was a business trip, because she really had no intentions of bringing back any business directly to the firm. If Dimitri would however, invest $200 million with Javier, Jennifer as well as Tate Yardley would certainly be richly rewarded.

Friday morning, Javier personally drove Jennifer to the airport. They were both quite excited about her upcoming trip. "Bellissima, you are my best ambassador. I know you will convince him to invest with us. And by the way, from what Mercedes tells me the $200 million is just the tip of the iceberg. And most importantly," he handed her a brown envelope, "this is the paper he needs to sign to wire his funds to us. Whatever happens, make sure he signs this paper. He also told Mercedes that if all goes well, he has other Russian friends who would like to invest with us."

As he drove the car on the tarmac to the waiting jet, he squeezed her hand. "My darling I truly love you and will desperately miss you. When you come back, I I have a big surprise planned." While they were still in the car, he reached over and gave her one of his long passionate kisses. Two members of the crew in white and blue uniforms came over to carry the luggage to the plane.

As Jennifer got out of the car, the wind was blowing her flaxen blond hair. The captain came over to inform them that they would be ready for takeoff just as soon as the jet was fueled up. Javier asked him if they would be making any stops for fuel before arriving at their destination. "No sir, this Gulfstream is equipped with wing tip tanks, so we will be flying directly to the Nice airport. And sir, don't worry about your lady friend, she's in good hands with us. Miss, I suggest that you step aboard so the crew can acquaint you with the cabin."

Jennifer looked longingly at Javier. "You know, in all this time I've never told you that I love you. Javier, you mean the world to me. I'm looking forward to this adventure, but also can't wait to come back home to you. I truly love you." She hugged and kissed him, breathing in his scent so it would stay etched in her memory.

Holding hands tightly he walked her to the steps of the plane and gave here one more kiss. "Ciao bella, have a wonderful trip. Please call me when you have safely landed."

Jennifer turned and headed up the stairs. She felt exhilaration as well as a sense of anxiousness. As she entered the cabin, a pretty young stewardess welcomed her aboard. "Miss Palmer, I'd like to show you around." The interior was outfitted with six large blue and gray leather swivel seats. There were two flat screen TV monitors facing the seats. "This is the general seating area but here is a bedroom where you might like to take a nap after we serve lunch." The room was small, but contained a round bed covered with a cream-colored duvet piled high with navy blue pillows. The stewardess then opened a door. "And here is your private bathroom with shower where you might like to freshen up before we land." Jennifer had traveled most of her life but never in such luxury. She thought that after an experience like this, commercial travel would never be the same. "The captain needs your passport to present to French customs upon our arrival. Why don't you give it to me now, so we won't have to disturb you later? After landing, I'll make sure it's returned to you."

They walked back to the main seating area where Jennifer selected a seat right behind the galley. Looking up at the stewardess, she asked, "Will anyone else be joining us on the trip?"

"No Miss Palmer, Mr. Dimitri sent his jet only to pick you up."

The captain came back and told Jennifer that they were cleared for take-off. The stewardess handed her a menu. "After we reach a comfortable cruising speed, please select anything you would like. We just picked up some beautiful jumbo shrimp for an appetizer at the seafood market and my crewmate makes a mean cocktail sauce. Before we take off, what may I get you to drink? How about a glass of Cristal?"

Even though it wasn't even 11:00 a.m., Jennifer thought that a champagne toast was a perfect idea. "Thank you, that sounds wonderful." Just as she took her first sip of the icy champagne, Jennifer heard the roar of the engines and felt the plane start to move. She looked out the window and was surprised to see that Javier's car was gone. She knew that he probably had important matters to take care of at the office. Before she knew it, the jet was aloft. Jennifer glanced out at the cumulus clouds, and felt a sense of embarking on a great adventure.

Since the cabin was starting to get a bit chilly, Jennifer got up to retrieve a pashmina from her carry-on bag. The stewardess came out of the galley. "Miss Palmer, you might be more comfortable with this," she said, handing her a white fox throw. Yes, Jennifer agreed, the throw was definitely more comfortable than her flimsy little pashmina. Settling into her seat, she felt a large pocket on the outside of the armrest. Digging into it, she found a Kindle, an IPad and an Ipod, along with a remote control for the flat screen TV. She turned on the power button and an image of the world appeared showing a bright blue dot where their plane was currently located. Above the map was a log showing the miles flown thus far vs. the total mileage to their final destination as well as a measurement of their current altitude and temperature outside. Jennifer pressed on the channel button and was able to get CNN, CNBC and all the other major networks and cable stations. When she pressed the DVD button, a catalogue of current movies came up from which she could select. For starters, Jennifer put on CNBC so at least she would have an idea of what was going on in the financial markets. She then took a look at the menu. It offered a wide array of tasty delicacies. She decided to follow the stewardess's suggestion of jumbo shrimp for an appetizer. For the main course, she chose Maine lobster stuffed with crabmeat, served with new potatoes and asparagus. At this point, she couldn't even think about dessert. After giving the stewardess her order, she closed her eyes and made a special prayer thanking God for giving her all the blessings in her life. She was so grateful for all that she had.

The sound of the engine lulled her into a light sleep only to be awakened by the smell of food cooking in the galley. The stewardess came by with the shrimp cocktail. "We saw that you were sleeping and didn't want to disturb you earlier." She brought over a teak table on which she placed a white starched tablecloth, shiny silver utensils and the appetizer. Even though Jennifer rarely had lunch, she found that she was voraciously hungry. The crewmate came by and offered her a selection of wines. She chose a Pouilly Fuisse to accompany the lobster. A short time later, the stewardess brought over a plate of the lobster, cleanly taken out of its shell surrounding a centerpiece of crab stuffing. She again came back with a platter of vegetables. Jennifer touched DVD on the remote control button and selected Woody Allen's "Midnight in Paris," and dined on her delicious luncheon.

After clearing the plates, the stewardess brought over a dessert menu complete with crepes, chocolate mousse and a variety of gelatos. Jennifer couldn't eat another bite. In fact, she was planning on taking advantage of the bedroom. While dozing on and off during the movie, Jennifer finally got herself up and went into the bedroom. The stewardess stuck her head in. "Miss Palmer, just press the button by the bed if there is anything we can do for you, otherwise I'll leave you alone to rest. Just so you know, we should be arriving in Nice around 12 midnight their time. That's in about six hours, so you'll have plenty of time to rest. Sweet dreams." Jennifer looked around the room and found a satin bathrobe to change into. Immediately getting into bed and under the covers, she fell into a deep slumber.

It seemed as though only minutes had passed when there was a knock at the door. It was the stewardess. "Miss Palmer, we will be landing in about 45 minutes. If you'd like to take a shower to freshen up, please feel free to do so. Otherwise, French customs will be coming onboard right after we park and you need to be in your seat in case they have any questions."

Jennifer had been to Europe many times in her life, but this was the fastest and most comfortable trip she had ever taken. Instead of taking a shower, she washed her face and brushed her teeth in the bathroom and took advantage of the toiletries that were offered next to the vanity. Within twenty minutes she was revitalized and sitting up in her seat looking forward to the next step of her adventure.

The plane landed soon after and customs did come on board for a perfunctory inspection. The captain and co-pilot came out to return her passport and wish her well as did the stewardess and first mate. The captain told her that Mr. Dimitri's personal driver was waiting for her on the tarmac and that her bags were already placed securely in the car. Jennifer looked at her watch, it was exactly midnight. Walking down the steps of the plane, she saw the silhouette of a limousine with a burly man standing next to it, awaiting her arrival. He immediately walked over to Jennifer and in a thick Russian accent said, "Miss Palmer, I am Igor, your driver. I will take you to Mr. D's yacht." He opened the back door for her. Before getting into the car, she looked back longingly at the jet, now bathed in a sea of light, against the dark sky. At least she had a sense of security on the plane. Now, she was in a foreign country, in the middle of the night, with a fellow named Igor, driving her who knows where. What was she thinking when she accepted the offer of this trip? Obviously, it was way too late to back out now. The die had been cast. Reluctantly, she slipped into her seat. After Igor settled into the driver's seat, he asked, "Miss Palmer, you want drink?"

"No, Igor, I'm fine." She knew from her previous vacations to the south of France, that the trip would take one and a half hours. She recalled that when she and her family would spend the high season in St. Tropez, with all the tourist traffic, the trip could easily take over three hours. But at this time of night, there probably wasn't a soul on the road. Within minutes the car was on Autoroute A8, speeding through the night. As time passed, Jennifer was getting more apprehensive. She pulled out her I-phone from her bag and decided to call Javier. She knew that he would calm her nerves. Even though it was past 6:00 p.m., he was probably still in the office.

After three rings, he answered the phone, "Cordova here."

"Javier, it's me, we just landed in Nice and I need to talk to you. I feel spooked out being here."

"Bellissima, it's wonderful to hear your voice. I'm so glad that you arrived safely. My darling, don't be frightened, you are in the best of hands. Mercedes is a good friend of Dimitri's and she was just telling me today, what a wonderful host he is. From what she said, you will be treated royally and the best part is that you will be mixing a little business with a lot of pleasure. Remember my darling, a $200 million investment by Dimitri, can afford you anything of your dreams."

"I know, Javier; I just feel uncomfortable here all alone and miss you. It would be so much better if you were with me."

"My darling, please relax. You're only going to be away for a few days. Just enjoy it. I have to let you go now, because I'm due at a dinner meeting with one of my largest investors. Just remember that I love you."

Even though Javier abruptly cut their conversation off, hearing his voice made Jennifer feel better, especially since it seemed from what he had said that Mercedes knew Dimitri so well. She decided to take Javier's advice and relax.

An hour later, the car veered off at the exit to St. Tropez, "Cannet des Meures." They would probably be arriving into the city within minutes.

Sure enough, 15 minutes later, the car pulled up to the St. Tropez Port. Igor got out, opened her door and then popped open the trunk to gather her belongings. He then proceeded to take her luggage to a launch that was tied up next to the dock. Two men in black and white striped t-shirts, black pants and black berets approached Jennifer. The taller one introduced himself. "Miss Palmer, I am Francois, this is Boris. We are here to take you to "The Stoli." Noticing Jennifer's perplexed look, he added, "We must anchor offshore because "The Stoli" is well over 60 meters long."

Igor had finished placing Jennifer's luggage on the launch and had driven away. Francois held out his hand to Jennifer. "Miss Palmer, may I help you aboard?" Jennifer took his hand and stepped onto the launch. Francois guided her inside. "Mademoiselle, I think you might be more comfortable in here, it is a bit chilly tonight." He then went back outside and unleashed the boat from the dock. Boris was at the controls and started up the engine. Moments later they were speeding across the inky sea heading toward "The Stoli."

Before she knew it, the launch slowed down its speed to an idle and parked next to a massive yacht, resembling a huge dark wedding cake. Since it still was the dead of night, Jennifer could barely make out the features of the ship. All she could tell was that the launch was dwarfed by its size. Two more men in the same uniforms as Francois and Boris were waiting on the embarkation deck. While Boris kept the launch steady, Francois passed Jennifer's luggage to one of the men. The other helped her navigate her way aboard the yacht. Once on board, he told her that since everyone was still sleeping, he would show her directly to her cabin. They took a small elevator up to Deck 2 and headed toward mid-ship. Halfway down the corridor he stopped and opened the cabin door for Jennifer. The room was all lit up. The curtains were drawn and on a small table was a beautiful bouquet of fresh flowers in a cut crystal vase with a fruit basket. Jennifer picked up a folded card in front of the flowers, it read, "Welcome Jennifer. Please treat this as your home. Looking forward to seeing you in the morning." It was signed "D."

The crew member placed her luggage in the cabin, and asked if there would be anything else she would need. After traveling for over 10 hours, all Jennifer wanted was to take a hot shower and plop into bed. She thanked him and told him that she was fine. Before closing the cabin door, he said, "Miss Palmer, breakfast is served at 9:00 a.m. and Mr. D will be looking forward to seeing you then. Please dial #11 on the house phone if you find that you need anything before then. Good night."

Jennifer was relieved to finally be alone. She sat on the bed and took in her surroundings. The room was apparently decorated with the height of decadence in mind. Three of the walls were mirrored as was the ceiling. The high bed was covered with a gold threaded comforter. There were two Louis XIV nightstands, topped with golden lamps. At the foot of the bed was a Jacuzzi tub. Jennifer walked into the bathroom. It was a vision of green marble. The twin sinks were gold as was all the hardware. Jennifer was so exhausted from her travels that she turned on the multi-headed shower, took off her clothes, leaving them on the marble floor and entered the shower.

The hot water was a welcome relief splashing over her body, releasing the tension that had built up inside her during the day. Jennifer luxuriated with the Bulgari soaps and shampoos that were attractively displayed in a cove of the shower stall. After turning off the water, she reached for towels from a nearby stand. To her surprise, they were heated. She wrapped one around her hair and one around her taut nude body. Without even bothering to unpack or search for her nightgown, she made her way to the bed, lifting the comforter and slipping between the sheets. A button by the bed turned off all the lights in the cabin. The gentle rocking of the yacht quickly lulled her into a deep slumber.

Chapter 31

A ringing bell interrupted Jennifer's sleep. She thought that she was still dreaming. Groggily, she opened her eyes to get her bearings and remembered that she wasn't at home but on a yacht in the middle of the Mediterranean. The bell was a phone next to her bedside. Lazily, reaching over to answer it, she heard a man's voice, "Miss Palmer, just wanted to inform you that it is half past eight in the morning and Mr. D is looking forward to seeing you at 9:00 breakfast which is being served on the fantail, Deck One."

Jennifer got the message, loud and clear. Literally leaping out of bed, she ran to the shower to wake up. After a quick rinse, she dug out her cosmetic bag, adroitly applying enough blush, mascara and lipstick to look presentable. She pulled back her hair into a ponytail, grabbed a pink Canovas sundress out of her luggage and with no time to spare headed out of her cabin. Taking the elevator up one deck, it opened to a beautifully furnished salon. A waiter in a white uniform was rushing by when he saw Jennifer. "Miss Palmer, Mr. D is expecting you, please come with me."

She followed him out two automatic doors into the bright sunlight. Immediately she saw the large figure of Dimitri sitting at a table under a yellow umbrella. As soon as he saw her, he got up and walked toward her with open arms. "The beautiful Jennifer has finally arrived." He gave her a big hug. Gently taking her arm he said, "Please, come sit down. You must be hungry. We have plenty of food and whatever we don't have, we can get for you."

Jennifer sat down next to him at the table, which was set up with beautiful china and crystal. To their right was a large buffet laden with fruits, cheeses, cold meats and all types of baked goods. Next to the table was a griddle where the chef was making eggs. The server came over and asked Jennifer what she would like for breakfast. Since she hadn't had a bite since lunch the previous day on the jet, she was starving. "I'd like a spinach and cheese omelet with hash brown potatoes and a bowl of berries."

"And to drink, Miss?"

"I'd like a glass of grapefruit juice and a club soda, thank you."

"Now beautiful Jennifer, aren't you happy to finally be here? This is my paradise at sea. We have everything on The Stoli, a beautiful gym, a cinema with the latest American movies, a bowling alley, a beauty salon as well as the best chefs to prepare anything you could ever desire. And, look at this day, the sky is blue, the sun is shining and there you can see St. Tropez."

Jennifer had to admit that the setting was breathtaking; and it was wonderful to be on such a luxurious yacht in the Mediterranean, off the shore of one of her favorite destinations. The only thing missing was to be sharing the experience with Javier. Jennifer knew that the sooner she got him to sign the wire instructions, the sooner she would be on her way home. "So Dimitri, thank you for your kind hospitality. Your jet was fantastic. I felt as though I were on a flying on a magic carpet ride. I have to admit though that it was a little scary coming here in the dead of night."

"Beautiful Jennifer, there's nothing to be afraid of. I will take good care of you."

Jennifer's breakfast arrived and she actually was too hungry to speak. Dimitri just watched her with a big smile on his face. After she finally finished possibly the best omelet she had ever tasted, she thought it might be a good time to discuss business. But Dimitri seemed to have other ideas. "Jennifer, we talk business later, now I want to give you a tour of my big boat."

They both stood up and he took her hand. "Come, I will show you." He then proceeded to take Jennifer on a tour of the yacht from Deck One to Deck Eight. In a word, Jennifer found it to be the epitome of conspicuous consumption. Everything that looked like gold actually was. There were two helicopters on the top deck. Dimitri took her into the belly of the yacht that opened up like a huge garage to the sea, where there were all types of recreational watercraft as well as three launches to take guests ashore. The engine room was a high tech marvel. Jennifer was expecting to see a huge wheel that the captain would use to steer the yacht. Instead, there were computers that navigated the boat without the captain being there all the time as well as radar and sonar to alert the crew of inclement weather or unwelcome guests. Dimitri told her that for security, he had hired ex Mosad officers to protect the yacht and its guests.

The last stop on the tour was his bedroom suite. Jennifer started to get a little apprehensive as they entered the suite. "This, beautiful Jennifer, is where I play and sleep." The room was almost half the size of a deck. Like her cabin, it had floor to ceiling mirrors and a huge round bed in the center. Several flat screen monitors were hung on the wall. One was showing the activity on the upper deck. Jennifer wondered what the others might reveal. "Beautiful Jennifer, do you like my suite?" He started to approach her personal space and she knew that she had to stop him in a nice way.

"Dimitri, it's a pity to waste such a beautiful day, why don't we go back to the upper deck and soak in the sun? I'll run up to my cabin and put on a bathing suit and then we can talk further."

Before Dimitri could say another word, Jennifer was off to her cabin feeling lucky to get away from a bear of a man. As she was changing into her one-piece suit, she thought that after an hour or so in the sun, she could approach him about business. Grabbing a hat and her cover up she took the elevator back up to the top deck.

Sure enough, he was waiting there for her in swimming trunks and his big hairy chest. He suggested that they sit by the pool that had a magnificent fountain splashing in the center. Surrounding the pool were two whirlpools, one hot and one cold. The crisp morning chill had given way to the warmth of the sun. As soon as Jennifer sat down, a crew member, dressed in the same black and white striped T-shirts that she had remembered from last night, helped her get situated on the chaise with fluffy yellow towels and a pillow for her head. "What would Miss Palmer care to drink?" he asked. Even though the Bloody Mary looked great, Jennifer opted for a Pellegrino with lime. She knew that she wanted to keep her brain clear, so she could accomplish her mission of having Dimitri sign the money transfer papers. When her water arrived in an iced silver bucket, the waiter poured her a glass and Dimitri held up his drink. "To my new American girlfriend."

Jennifer was taken aback by his toast, but forcing a smile, held up her glass to his. She laid her head back on the lounge chair, soaking in the reflection of the sun on the turquoise sea. Within moments, she felt a hairy leg rub up against her silky body. Dimitri had come over to share her lounge chair. Trying to be diplomatic, she said, "Dimitri, you're going to ruin my tan. Go back over to your chair and behave." Surprisingly, like a dog with his tail between his legs, he obediently obeyed her command. Relieved, she thought that now might be an ideal time to discuss business. "Dimitri, on your personal request, I traveled all the way over here from South Florida. As you can imagine, I am a very busy lady. But I promised you at Mercedes' party that I would come. And a promise is a promise. I'm sure Mercedes told you about the business, in which I am involved. And, as you have undoubtedly read, the U.S. equity markets have been quite volatile as of late. However, now might be the ideal time in which to invest. I have a close connection to a money manager that has made money for his clients in good times as well as bad. You would be quite pleased with his performance."

"My beautiful Jennifer, it would be a pleasure to invest with you. That way, I would have an excuse to see you many times a year. Yes, it would be a very good idea, my lapushka. What would you think if I first invest $100 million US? And depending on your performance, in more ways than one, I might double it."

Jennifer had been expecting a $200 million investment up front. But really, who was she to quibble with $100 million? After Javier would work his magic and show Dimitri high returns he would definitely wire over more funds. "Dimitri, I am so pleased that you would like to invest with us," she said pulling out the papers from her bag, "I just need a little information to open an account for you and your signature for authorization to wire funds to our U.S. bank."

"My beautiful Jennifer, let's not be in such a rush. Why not enjoy this beautiful day? How about we continue this nuisance business over lunch later? I want to learn more about the beautiful Jennifer."

Jennifer realized that if she pushed him too hard he would back away. So, the best thing to do was to appease him and have a pleasant conversation. She let him do most of the talking, asking him about his early life and the workings of his vodka company. She found that once she got him on a roll, he couldn't stop talking about himself. During their conversation he must have consumed at least three Bloody Marys. She just laid her head back on the lounge chair, soaking in the sun and pretending to listen intently to his stories. At noon, the same crewmate who had served them breakfast came around and announced that lunch had been prepared and was waiting for them on the fantail. Jennifer noticed that by this time, Dimitri's speech was a little bit slurred and it took him a couple of tries to elevate himself from the chaise. Now that he was a bit tipsy, she felt confident that he would sign her papers over lunch.

Leaning on her for support, they made their way to the fantail where a delectable buffet had been set up. There were all types of antipastos and salads available along with gravlax, crabmeat, grilled shrimp, octopus and a variety of marinated vegetables. At the end of the display of food, there was a cornucopia of fruits and freshly baked baguettes and rolls. Jennifer never experienced this standard of service before, except maybe at the Ritz or Four Seasons. She really couldn't believe that an individual could live on such a high level.

They each had a waiter that carried their plates to the table. As much as Jennifer was looking forward to going home, it wouldn't take very much to get used to this lifestyle. The waiter poured white wine with their lunch. Since Dimitri was also eating, he was able to maintain an intelligent conversation. After clearing their plates, the waiter came by with a freezer on wheels containing various flavors of homemade gelatos and sorbets. They each selected two scoops.

While they were eating their desserts, Jennifer felt it would be appropriate to rekindle their previous business discussion. "My beautiful Jennifer, I will sign your papers, as long as you promise to stay for the party tonight. I want to show you off to my friends. Then if you wish, you may return back to the States tomorrow afternoon. I will make sure that my jet will be available to safely take you back home. Do we have a deal?" he said with a twinkle in his eye.

Jennifer couldn't have been happier. "Dimitri, it would be a pleasure to attend your party. Thank you for the invitation."

Finally he signed the papers, handing them back to her. "Now, my Jennifer, let's take a siesta."

Reading between the lines, Jennifer suggested that since they had just eaten, it might be better to go back in the sun and relax. To her relief, he agreed. No sooner had they returned to their lounge chairs, she heard him snoring away.

The server came by and asked her if there was anything she might like to have. She asked him what time the party was to start in the evening and if he could arrange for her to go ashore for a little sightseeing. He quietly motioned for her to follow him. Grabbing her bag with the signed documents safely inside, she followed him back to the deck where she had embarked the night before. In Russian, he spoke to one of the mates. Minutes later, a tender came up to the ship and Jennifer was helped on with two other burly Russians accompanying her. She told them that she knew St. Tropez well and didn't need any company. They notified her that Mr. D didn't want any of his guests leaving the ship without the accompaniment of his bodyguards.

Once the launch took off toward land, Jennifer pulled out her cell phone to call home. Immediately, one of the Russians walked over and took it out of her hands. "No phone calls now. We give to you later." Jennifer couldn't imagine why they would confiscate her cell phone. It wasn't as though she was privy to any secret information. She figured that once on land she would find a public phone. As they approached the shore, Jennifer spotted one of her favorite restaurants, the one with the blue awnings that had the best bouillabaisse in the South of France. She was excited to be back in St. Tropez.

Once the launch was secured dockside, Jennifer's two new "friends" helped her onto the wharf. Since they spoke limited English, they motioned for her to lead the way. After Bridget Bardot first planted her roots in St. Tropez, the city has long been an epicenter for the elite. The local paparazzi were continuously on the lookout for the latest celebrities. Sensing that Jennifer was someone "important," with two bodyguards in tow, the photographers gathered around the threesome like fruit flies snapping photos. Ignoring their presence, Jennifer made a beeline to her favorite boutiques. Sleek European sports cars cautiously made their way down the tourist filled streets.

Previously, Jennifer had originally intended to phone home on her cell to speak with her parents, her office and to relay the good news to Javier. However, since her "escorts" had temporarily confiscated her I-Phone, she had to resort to using a public phone. She decided to stop at a patisserie for a fresh baguette. While paying the cashier, she noticed a public phone just outside of the ladies room. She motioned to the two goons that she would be right back. Since they were each enjoying a French pastry and the sights of beautiful women walking by, they waved her off. Once at the phone, Jennifer successfully made a credit card call to her office. After getting through to her assistant, she had her conference the call to her parents' number. Her mother answered the phone and was thrilled to hear her daughter's voice. "Mom, I'm fine and still in St. Tropez but I'm expecting to fly back to the States tomorrow. I'll call you as soon as I land. Love and kisses to you and Daddy."

Since she knew that her assistant was on the phone, she didn't want to go further with the conversation. After hanging up with her mother, she asked to be conferenced in with Javier. It was only 5:30 p.m., so she assumed that he was still in the office. After several rings, his secretary answered his personal line. When Jennifer asked to speak with him, she told her that Javier was meeting with Mercedes and asked not to be interrupted. Pleadingly, Jennifer said, "But just tell him it's me, I'm sure he'll take the call. And I know that Mercedes would like to hear from me as well."

"Miss Palmer, please understand, I don't want to lose my job for ignoring his request. As soon as they finish, I will tell him that you called and I'm sure he will phone you right back." Jennifer could tell that arguing with the woman would be a losing proposition, so dejectedly she hung up, knowing that when Javier would call she wouldn't have her phone. As expected, the two goons were waiting for her to return in the shop. Pissed at not being able to get through to Javier, she walked out to the street without acknowledging her chaperones. Immediately, they leapt out of their seats to follow Jennifer. She knew that the only way to deal with her disappointment was to focus on a little retail therapy. After a couple of hours of shopping, Jennifer was informed that they needed to head back to the yacht. The threesome walked to the dock. At least the two guys served some purpose by carrying the shopping bags from the various boutiques where Jennifer had made her purchases.

The launch was waiting with its engine running ready to whisk the group back in time for the party. During the trip, Jennifer heard her cell phone ring. Assuming that it was Javier, she attempted to communicate to the Russian that she needed to answer her phone. He was totally unresponsive. Either he didn't understand, which would have been totally moronic, or he didn't want to comprehend, which was more likely the case. At worst, Jennifer would get her phone back tomorrow and call Javier on the way to the airport. As they approached "The Stoli," one could sense an air of excitement. From the distance, you could see a bright yellow canvas that had been stretched over the top deck, where the party would be. Various boats were moored next to the yacht. There was an open boat, full of prepared flower arrangements that were being brought on board. There were two others containing provisions of food and liquor. Jennifer's launch barely found space between the others to allow her back on. Since the crew mates were rushing around, getting things in ship-shape, one of the bodyguards helped her with the shopping bags, walking her back to her cabin. Before he left, she asked, "Will you give me my phone back now?" Reluctantly, he handed her phone back to her.

Jennifer had two hours to prepare for the party and wanted to make the best of the time available. She thought about phoning Javier back, but decided against it since he had blocked her call earlier. Let him wonder what was happening. Since he was so pre-occupied earlier, she would make him wait through the night to hear from her. Before taking a steam and a shower, she packed up her belongings for the trip home tomorrow, leaving out a yellow jersey Lauren gown for that evening and an outfit for the next day. She took out of her purse, the money transfer form that Dimitri had finally signed earlier in the day. Jennifer knew that no matter what, that signed document wasn't going to leave her side. In fact, before she forgot, she would put it in her Leiber evening bag along with her cell phone.

After finally getting dressed for the party, she opened her cabin door only to find the two goons waiting for her. One said to her with a broken toothed smile, "We take you to party." Knowing that this lunacy would be over tomorrow, Jennifer resigned herself to going with them to the party upstairs. By the time they arrived, it was already in full swing. The pool had been transformed into a dance floor. There was a five piece orchestra playing disco rhythms. The guests were mostly young girls with a few men sprinkled into the assortment. While walking across the deck, Jennifer overheard conversations in French, Spanish, Russian and even a little English. There was a lavish array of food. She saw Dimitri, in a navy blue smoking jacket and open light blue silk shirt with his signature diamond medallion hanging from his hairy chest. She went over to greet him. Pleased to see her, he kissed her hand and pulled her closer to him, giving her a wet kiss on the lips. He proudly introduced her as his money manager from America to the circle of friends around him.

From the corner of Jennifer's eye, she could see a small black rubber dinghy approaching the yacht. She supposed that it was probably a guest making a fashionably late entrance. Within minutes though, all havoc was breaking loose. Three men in wetsuits, carrying guns were on the deck, shouting commands in French that everyone lay down on the deck. Jennifer knew that Dimitri liked drama, but she quickly figured out that this wasn't part of the evening's planned festivities. Since she had been standing behind the bridge, the band of "pirates" had not spotted her. She however, had looked over the side of the boat to where their dinghy was tied up. Determined not to become a willing hostage, she rushed down the back steps of the yacht to where the dinghy was secured. As she ran down, she was thinking about what she would be leaving in her cabin. She was wearing the jewelry she had brought, so basically all that was left was her passport, a little cash and her clothes. She had the most important item with her, Dimitri's money transfer agreement as well as her phone. Once the funds were moved to Cordova, she could easily afford to buy all the clothes in the world.

All she knew right now was that she had to get away. Finally making it to the lowest deck, she pulled up her dress and lowered herself into the dinghy. To her relief, the key to the ignition was left in the little boat. She turned it on and the engine roared to life. Holding the rudder tightly in her right hand and her evening bag in her left, she pointed the little dinghy's bough toward the shoreline. The sun had just set, leaving a darkened sky. The moon provided just enough reflection off the sea, along with the lights of the shore to help Jennifer navigate her way.

She knew that she had to phone Javier and let him know what was happening. While still steering the dinghy, she maneuvered her phone out of her purse and was able to speed dial Javier. Happily, he answered the phone, and before he had a chance to speak she said, "Javier, something weird is going down on that ship. I am escaping from a group of pirates with guns. I'm just getting to the shore. Please do whatever you can to help me. I have to go."

Moments later, she heard a helicopter circling right above her. Someone on "The Stoli" must have been able to get away and alert the authorities. But instead of flying over to the yacht, the helicopter hovered over Jennifer, directing a spotlight on her as she was speeding toward the dock. Minutes later, she made it to the safety of the harbor only to be met by the local police. She was so happy to see them after her ordeal. Getting herself out of the dinghy, they shouted at her in French with guns drawn to raise her arms in the air and not to move. She tried to explain to them about what was taking place on the yacht and how she had gotten away.

Ignoring her words, they approached her, taking her handbag and handcuffing her small wrists behind her back. She was shouting at them, that she had done nothing wrong. That she was just fleeing a dangerous situation. Ignoring her protestation, with her arms secured behind her, they led her to a waiting police car. Jennifer felt as though she were living a nightmare. What the hell was going on? Once they got to the station, she would hopefully be able to explain her situation to a supervisor with a brain.

Chapter 32

After the patrol car pulled into the station, the paparazzi were awaiting their arrival. As Jennifer stepped out of the car, there was a flood of flashes, blinding her way. A gendarme was on either side of her guiding her quickly into the station house. Jennifer still couldn't believe the predicament she was in. At least hopefully, someone here would listen to her story. Making their way inside, several men in plain clothes were speaking on the phone. After taking off her handcuffs, without stopping, the gendarmes placed her in a cell beside the entrance. Since she could hear and understand what the men on the phone were saying, she figured out that she was imminently about to be transferred to Nice. From what she could make out, she heard the French word for money laundering and they seemed to keep referring to Interpol and the FBI.

Jennifer recalled how the judicial system in many countries outside of the U.S. presumed you to be guilty after an arrest. She shouted out, "Someone please come here. You need to listen to what I have to say. I haven't done anything wrong. Just please get me out of here. I want to go home." Jennifer started sobbing out of fear and frustration.

Finally, one of the men came over to her cell and said in broken English, "We are transferring you to Nice tonight. Interpol and the Unites States FBI are waiting there to speak with you and hear your story. You are the first prisoner we have had here in over ten years. We are not equipped to handle a situation of this magnitude and they want to speak to you, personally."

"Please, I have done nothing wrong. I am an innocent person. This is all a terrible misunderstanding. Please listen to me. I beg you. Let me speak to a U.S. diplomat here. Don't I at least get a phone call? I need my handbag. Where is it?"

"Mademoiselle that will all be taken care of in Nice. Please be patient. You will be leaving shortly."

Jennifer realized that all her evening bag contained was a little cash, a credit card, her cell phone and most importantly the money transfer authorization document with Dimitri's signature. She didn't even have her driver's license. Moments later, two other men approached her cell, unlocking it and taking her by the arm to another squad car, placing her in the back seat and slamming the door shut. She attempted to open the door, but it had been secured. The two men got into the front seat; one was holding a brown envelope that looked to be containing her handbag. With the siren blaring, the car sped toward the city of Nice.

The night air had turned chilly and all Jennifer was wearing was her yellow jersey gown. "J'ai froid," she said. The man on the passenger side took off his jacket and handed it back to her. "Merci, Monsieur." Even though Jennifer's adrenaline was on high alert, she knew that any conversation with the officials occupying the front seat would be futile. So she resigned herself to quietly waiting out the trip to Nice.

Between the lack of heavy traffic and the police siren, they made it to Nice within the hour. Pulling the car up to a regal looking edifice, the man on the passenger side jumped out, speaking rapidly into his phone. He opened Jennifer's door, taking her arm and leading her into the building to a conference room on the second floor. A youngish clean-cut man in shirtsleeves was sitting at the table. When Jennifer and her guard walked into the room, the man got up, extending his hand to her and saying with an American accent, "Miss Palmer, we have been looking forward to meeting you. Please have a seat. Would you care for anything to drink?"

Jennifer was just so relieved to finally see an American that she shook her head and started to sob uncontrollably.

"Miss Palmer, my name is Inspector Healey, I'm with the FBI. My counterparts with Interpol are here as well to interrogate you. This is going to be a long night; I suggest you take advantage of my offer for a beverage. I'll have an iced tea brought in for you."

"You have no idea how happy I am to see you. There has been a huge misunderstanding."

"Wait, Miss Palmer, even though we are in France, you will be extradited back to South Florida when we finish. It is my responsibility to read you your Miranda Rights before you speak."

While he was reading her rights under U.S. law, Jennifer still couldn't fathom what was happening. Interrupting him she said, "What have I done wrong? Why are you arresting and extraditing me? What the hell is happening here? Someone please help me!"

Completing the dissertation of the Miranda Rights, Inspector Healy finally looked up at Jennifer, who was again sobbing uncontrollably. "Miss Palmer, you are under arrest for International Money Laundering as well as Financial Fraud. You and your cohorts have been our primary focus for the past four months."

"International Money Laundering, what on earth on you talking about?"

"Miss Palmer, before we continue, you do have a right to an attorney. Would you like us to bring in an attorney?"

"No, I don't need an attorney. I haven't done anything wrong. Let me just explain to you what has happened."

Healy took a paper out of his file and showed it to her. "Miss Palmer, this was found in your possession. Do you recognize it?"

"Yes," she answered.

"Do you know a Dimtri Stravinsko?"

"Yes, I just escaped off his yacht from a band of pirates."

"Miss Palmer, those weren't pirates. They were our contacts at Interpol. Their mission was to take you and Mr. Stravinsko into custody."

"For what?"

"This signed document you had in your handbag would have facilitated the laundering of hundreds of millions of dollars in the United States."

"No it wouldn't. Dimitri wanted to invest with us."

"Miss Palmer, do you know a Javier Cordova?"

"Yes."

"What do you know about him?"

"Javier is a highly acclaimed money manager. Inspector Healy, I've known him for over a year. He is a forthright and honorable man. What is your point?"

"The point, Miss Palmer is that Javier Cordova has mastered one of the largest Ponzi schemes since Madoff. And the point is that you are an accomplice of his. Now, Miss Palmer, do you get my point?"

"How is that possible?"

"Miss Palmer, you were set up to assist him in finding innocent victims who were looking for large returns on their investments. You were his front man, or rather, woman. Since you were working at the legitimate firm of Tate Yardley, you were the perfect pawn for his scheme. You were the bait. The investors would meet and trust you and then you would turn them over to Cordova Investments."

"But, Javier couldn't have been stealing their money. He invested their assets through me."

"Those transactions only represented less than 1 percent of the dollars he had accumulated. He wanted to keep you happy so you would continue feeding him more clients. Miss Palmer, I can't emphasize enough to you that this is a major Federal offense. If you are found guilty as an accomplice, you could face a maximum of twenty-five years in a Federal Penitentiary."

"Jail?" she said. "I would go to jail?"

"Yes, you would, that is unless you turn State's witness."

"What does that mean?"

"If you sign a paper tonight, agreeing to testify against Mr. Cordova, you would receive complete immunity and be able to continue on with your life. You must understand, if you are sentenced, you may not get out of jail until you are in your fifties. That would certainly be a waste of your young life."

"I couldn't possibly testify against him. I love him and I know he loves me. He was only trying to help me. I'm sure, if we can just get him on the phone, he will explain everything. He will clear this mess up. Inspector, I beg of you, please call him now."

"Miss Palmer, we have solid evidence against Mr. Cordova. There is no mistake. Your boyfriend has been stealing and laundering money for years. And in regards to your love affair with him, do you know Mercedes Cambridge?"

"Yes, she introduced us. She is one of the leading philanthropists in Palm Beach."

"Miss Palmer, are you aware that she and Mr. Cordova had been working together on this scheme? Your meeting with her was not by happenstance. They were searching for a young, naïve broker from a well-regarded brokerage firm to help them execute their plan. Mercedes

Cambridge was posing as a philanthropist, but in reality she has been a long-term con artist."

"You must be wrong. She's the widow of a wealthy steel magnate. In fact, I read in a magazine that she is one of the leading women in Palm Beach."

"Miss Palmer, that magazine that you are quoting from, was planted at the club where you first met Mrs. Cambridge. It was a phony mock-up put there purposely for you to see, to lend credibility to your meeting. Mrs. Cambridge is not even her real name. She has used several aliases over the years. Her real name is Mercedes Ortega. She moved to the States from Bogota where she was an exotic dancer. After securing her Green Card, she and Mr. Cordova have been hatching this Ponzi scheme for over a year and you Miss Palmer, fit them like a glove."

Jennifer was stunned. How could she have been so naive? She couldn't believe that Javier had deceived her and stolen her heart. Closing her eyes, she flashed back to the scenes of times they had spent together. Breaking down in tears again, she recalled the tender moments they shared making love. It had all been a lie. He used her in the worst possible way. Not only did he scar her emotionally, but he'd implicated her in a criminal offense. How was she going to ever explain this mess to her parents? They had been right all along, and she was just too blind to see. Through her tears, she looked up at the Inspector and said, "So what can I do now?"

"As I told you earlier, if you sign this paper, agreeing to testify against both of them, you will receive full immunity."

"What does that exactly mean?"

"Miss Palmer, you sign this paper tonight and you have the word of the U.S. Government that you will not be convicted in this matter. You will not go to jail. But understand that you must cooperate with us fully. We will fly you back to South Florida this evening, accompanied by one of our agents and you will be met at the airport by the local inspectors that have been following this case for the past year. You will provide them with any and all information they request and you will assist them in apprehending Mr. Cordova and Mrs. Cambridge. They will also make sure that you are protected and that no harm will come your way. You will also be obligated to testify against the two in court. Have I made myself clear? Miss Palmer, what do you choose to do?"

In a trembling voice, Jennifer responded, "I will sign your paper, but please let me call my parents."

He nodded in agreement, and then placed the document in front of Jennifer to sign. After she did, he requested that a phone be brought into the room. Taking the paper from her, he dialed her parents' number.

"How did you know what number to dial?"

"Miss Palmer, we are the FBI. We have records of all your phone numbers as well as all calls placed and received by you over the course of this investigation." He handed her the phone and stood up. "Miss Palmer, I will give you a few moments of privacy while you speak with your parents."

Handing her the phone, he left the room. Looking at her watch, she knew that her parents were probably just finishing dinner. Her father answered the phone. "Daddy, I need to speak with you both. I'm in trouble and I need your help."

She heard her father sending her mother to another extension. "Honey, where are you? What has happened?"

Her mother had picked up the phone. "Jennifer, baby, what is it?"

"Listen, I don't have much time. But right now I'm in Nice. The FBI arrested me."

"But what happened with the yacht you were supposed to be on?"

"Look, Mommy and Daddy, it's a long story. All I can say is that I was involved with some really bad people. You were right about Javier. Apparently he's a world class thief. And they were trying to implicate me with him. They told me that if I sign a paper and cooperate with them, I won't be convicted or go to jail. I just signed it and now they are going to fly me back home. They took my purse and all my belongings are still on the yacht. I don't have any money or my passport. I just need you both to support me through this and I think we need to hire an attorney. I should be home tomorrow and will fill you in on all the awful details. This has been a nightmare that just won't end." Starting to cry again she said, "I loved him so much. I had no idea that I was doing anything against the law. They told me that he's almost as bad as Madoff. I just can't believe that I fell in love with him."

"Jennifer," her father said, "we are always there for you. As soon as I hang up, we will get an attorney. We will help you through this. I still don't quite understand what happened, but you knew that we always thought Cordova was an unsavory character."

"Darling," her mother said, "are you all right? Have you been hurt in any way by the authorities?"

"No, Mom, physically I'm OK, it's just that I'm a mental wreck. I just want to go home."

Inspector Healy walked back in the room, looking at his watch.

"Mommy, Daddy they just came back in, I have to go. I'll call you again as soon as I can. I love you both."

Taking the phone from her, he said, "Monsieur Tatou from Interpol would like to have a few words with you and then we've gathered some clothes for you to change into for the flight home. We need to get you on the 6:00 a.m. flight, direct to Miami, so that only gives us a little more than an hour left for the interrogation."

After meeting with the man from Interpol, a female FBI agent came into the room. "Miss Palmer, I'm Inspector Grimes. Here are some basic clothes for you to change into and then I will accompany you back to South Florida."

"But Inspector, all of my possessions are still on the yacht. I don't even have my passport."

"Miss Palmer, you'll have to forego your possessions for now and we have arranged for you to re-enter the United States without your passport. Now go and change out of that gown, we have a plane to catch."

Inspector Grimes led Jennifer to a ladies room. Finally alone, Jennifer looked at her image in the mirror. She still couldn't comprehend the mess she had gotten herself into. Breaking down into tears again, she slowly managed to take off her yellow gown and change into a plain white button down shirt and navy skirt that had been provided to her. She had also been given a blue cardigan and black ballet flat-type shoes. The outfit looked like it was a uniform from a boarding school. Surprisingly everything seemed to fit. After folding her gown and placing it in the bag she walked out to where Inspector Grimes was waiting for her. As they made their way to the elevator, Inspector Healy came back out of his office. Extending his hand to her he said, "Miss Palmer, you will not regret signing the paper. By doing so, you have helped yourself as well as hundreds of innocent victims. Good luck to you."

Downstairs, a car was waiting to take them to the airport. Jennifer couldn't wait to get home.

Chapter 33

As the plane touched down at Miami International Airport, Jennifer felt relieved to finally be home. Even though she was home, she knew that she had several hurdles to cross, mainly, to cooperate with the FBI in apprehending Javier and Mercedes. After the exhaustion of the past 24 hours, she hoped that she could muster up the emotional strength to follow through on her "deal" with the government. The eight and a half hours of flying gave her a chance to think about what her supposed lover had done to her. How he had taken advantage of her in the most diabolical fashion. And to think, that he and Mercedes were together on this all along. Jennifer couldn't imagine how she never saw through it. The only answer that she could give herself was that she was simply in love. He seduced her in such a supreme way that she actually became putty in his hands. After much soul searching, Jennifer convinced herself that she would follow through and make these two con artists pay for the emotional damage they had done to her as well as conning hundreds of innocent investors.

Jennifer and Inspector Grimes were allowed to disembark before the other passengers. As they approached U.S. Customs, Grimes stepped ahead of Jennifer, speaking to the officer and showing him various documents. Jennifer was afraid to say a word, in fear that Customs might block her re-entry back into the country. Holding her breath, she saw the officer pull up her information on his computer. After what seemed like an eternity, he stamped the documents that Inspector Grimes had presented to him. As Jennifer walked past, he looked up and said, "Miss Palmer, welcome home." Hearing those words brought tears to Jennifer's eyes.

Since they had nothing to declare or luggage to inspect, the two women sailed through the remainder of the Customs process. Inspector Grimes was a woman that didn't mince words. During the flight back, she had barely conversed with Jennifer. Walking out of Customs into the humid Florida heat, she said to Jennifer, "Follow me to my car."

When they got to her white Ford Taurus, Jennifer looked at her and asked, "Where are we going now?"

"Miss Palmer, I am under strict orders not to let you out of my sight. I will be taking you home with me, where you will be safe, until we complete the investigation."

Jennifer was definitely not thrilled with this plan. "Miss Grimes, can't we at least stop at my parents' house? They have been so concerned about me. I just want them to see me and know that I'm in good hands."

Miss Grimes grimaced but accepted Jennifer's proposal. "All right, Miss Palmer, I'll take you to your parents' house as long as you don't reveal to them the scope of our investigation."

"I'll do whatever you say; I just want to see my parents."

The Inspector drove Jennifer to her parents' house. When they saw their daughter they were both overcome with emotion. Jennifer told them that she couldn't reveal the details of what was happening and Grimes assured them that their daughter would be safe with her. After a short visit, Grimes stated that they had to head out and told

Jennifer's parents that as soon as the investigation was complete, they would be able to have full access to their beloved daughter.

Once back in the car again, Jennifer asked if they could drive up to her apartment in Manalapan and gather some clothes and toiletries. Grimes responded, "Miss Palmer, we can't take the chance of anyone seeing you or putting your life at risk. Right now, the FBI will foot the bill for your expenses, including a reasonable cost for clothing and personal items. We have reason to believe that the two suspects you have been involved with have the ability and will to cause you bodily harm. It is my responsibility to keep you safe. Right now, we'll head over to my house where we will be met by another agent. Once you are settled in, we will write up a list of what you need and she will secure those items for you. Fair enough?"

"Miss Grimes, I didn't realize that I was in such a precarious situation. From what you are saying, I guess I really have no choice."

Grimes nodded and drove to her home. It was a modest nondescript little house. Very little landscaping and a lawn that looked like it was suffering from a lack of irrigation.

Once in the house, Jennifer found it to be neat and clean, but displaying no personality. There were no paintings on the white walls and no photos anywhere. Grimes ushered Jennifer to a small bedroom, furnished with a twin bed covered with a mauve colored bedspread, a bureau and a television. "This is where you will be staying. The bathroom is right outside this door." Handing Jennifer a pad and pen, she said, "Write up a list of the things you will need for the next few days. Agent Green should be here shortly."

Closing the bedroom door, Jennifer was standing in a bedroom the size of one of the guest bathrooms in her own apartment, with instructions to write a list for the things she would need. She couldn't stop thinking of what she had experienced over the past few days. What started out as a great adventure had turned into a true nightmare. Now she had to direct her energies against someone who had hurt her and others so badly.

Chapter 34

The next morning, Inspector Grimes awakened Jennifer. "Miss Palmer, please get dressed, we have to be at the local bureau in an hour. After you take a shower, please help yourself to orange juice and some toast in the kitchen." Jennifer took a quick shower and put on the clothes that had been brought for her the previous evening. They appeared to have been bought at the local Wal-Mart. She knew that there was no choice available to her but to go along with the program. She just wanted to get this over with and get on with her life.

They arrived at the FBI offices within the hour, where Inspector Handler met them. With him was an attorney, John Haskins, whom her parents had secured. Haskins requested that he have five minutes with Jennifer. Handler agreed and left them alone in the conference room. "Jennifer, your parents are extremely concerned about your welfare. How are you doing?"

"Mr. Haskins, the sooner we get this over with, the better. I can't take much more anxiety."

"Jennifer, I spoke at length with Inspector Handler, he told me that you are a crucial link to closing this case. He also assured me that once they apprehend your former associates you will be free to go home. Right now they are extremely concerned for your safety. Apparently, these people are notorious."

"Mr. Haskins, Javier was my lover, I can't believe he would do anything to cause harm to me."

"Jennifer, my best advice to you is to follow the agents' instructions. They are professionals and you must trust them. I will be here for you. So let's get on with it."

The attorney went out into the hallway to let Inspector Handler know that Jennifer was ready to proceed. When the inspector re-entered the room he was carrying a sealed package along with a file.

"Miss Palmer, please sit down. May I offer you some coffee?"

Jennifer shook her head.

"OK," he said. Opening the file, he pulled out two large photos. One of Javier and the other of Mercedes. "Miss Palmer, do you recognize this man and woman?"

"Yes, that is Javier Cordova and the woman is Mercedes Cambridge."

"All right, I would like you to call Mr. Cordova, now, and tell him you're back and how you can't wait to see him and tell him the good news. Offer to meet him at his house today. Let him know how much you missed him. I will give you back your cell phone so he will be unable to trace the call back to us. We will be monitoring the call, and since you have agreed to cooperate fully with us, you will not give him any reason to doubt you. Do you understand?"

"Yes sir." Jennifer was dying inside. She knew that she could be a good actress but this was above and beyond.

Inspector Handler dialed Javier's home number and handed the phone to Jennifer. Javier answered after the second ring.

"Javier," she said.

"Bellisima, it's wonderful to hear your voice. Where are you?"

"I'm back and can't wait to see you and tell you the good news. How long will you be home?"

"For you my darling, as long as you want. I can't wait to feel your body next to mine."

Jennifer looked at Inspector Handler; he was motioning with his hands to wrap it up and put up two fingers.

"Javier, how about if I come over by 11:00 a.m.?"

"Perfecto, mi amor, I'll be waiting for you. I have missed you desperately."

"I'll see you then."

After she hung up, Inspector Handler opened up the package he had brought into the room. It contained a long wire with what appeared to be a little speaker.

"Miss Palmer, Inspector Grimes will place this wire under your clothing. When you meet with Javier, this will allow us to hear your conversation. It is imperative that you have him describe as much as possible about what he is doing with the money he has raised. We are counting on you to have him incriminate himself so we can move in and arrest him. It is only fair to say that you will be in a dangerous situation. But we will be monitoring your every move. If there is any indication of imminent harm to you we will be prepared to act immediately. Are you ready for this undertaking?"

Jennifer drew a deep breath, and even though she was scared to death, she nodded that she was ready to move forward.

"Miss Palmer, so as not to arouse any suspicion on his part, we'll stop at your condominium, on the way to Palm Beach, to pick up your car. From there we will follow you to Mr. Cordova's house."

Handler called in Agent Grimes to attach the wire to Jennifer. He then led her out to the garage, where there were four unmarked cars waiting for them to make the drive up to Palm Beach. He, Jennifer and Grimes got into the first car. Within moments they were on the turnpike heading up to Palm Beach.

"Inspector Handler, since we are stopping off at my home to pick up the car, wouldn't it make sense for me to change into my own clothes? If Javier saw me dressed like this, he would probably think something was strange."

"All right, Miss Palmer, only I insist Agent Grimes escort you up to your apartment. We don't want to take any chances."

The drive up was quiet. Jennifer was deep in thought contemplating how she would pull this off. She felt intense fear, but at the same time remorse and sadness. She couldn't believe that she was on a mission to turn in her lover to the FBI. She had to keep in mind though, that it was he who had deceived her. He was a slick con artist who had taken advantage of her emotions.

When they pulled in to the condo garage, Agent Grimes escorted her up to the apartment. In a way, after being in her modest home, Jennifer felt a little embarrassed about the grandeur of her apartment. When she opened the door and went into her bedroom to change, she heard Grimes say to herself, "So this is how the other half lives." Jennifer relished the feeling of being home, but quickly changed so they would be on schedule. Before they left the apartment, Agent Grimes rechecked the wire to make sure it was on securely. She also handed Jennifer the document that Dimitri had signed. "You might need this."

Jennifer put it in her purse and grabbed the keys to the Aston Martin. They took the elevator back down to the garage. All four cars were waiting for them. Surprisingly, Agent Grimes said to her, "Miss Palmer, don't be afraid, I know this is extremely difficult for you to do, but we will have you covered all the way." She almost gave Jennifer a hug, but stopped herself and just patted her on the shoulder. Jennifer got into her car and the caravan made its way to Palm Beach.

By the time they approached Javier's house she was practically hyperventilating. She looked in her rear view mirror and saw that the four cars that had been following her had slipped into the side streets.

Driving up to the familiar gravel driveway, Jennifer parked her car. As she was getting out, she saw Javier come out the front door to greet her with open arms. Reluctantly, she walked over to him with a forced smile on her face and fell into his arms. "Bellisima, it is wonderful to see you. After your last call, I didn't know what happened to you."

Jennifer had forgotten that she had phoned him as she was escaping the yacht. "Oh," she said, "Dimitri was having a party, and I guess that I had too much to drink. I don't even remember what I was saying. But that doesn't matter; it's just great to be together again."

Javier lifted her chin up and kissed her passionately on the lips, gripping her body tightly against his. Despite it all, Jennifer felt the sensuous chill race through her body. Still, she was hoping that he wouldn't feel the wire wrapped under her dress. With his arm securely around her waist, they walked inside the house.

Javier walked over to the bar and poured them each a flute of Cristal and then motioned for her to sit next to him on the couch. He raised his glass and toasted her, "To my darling on her successful trip. We must never be apart again." As their glasses clinked, Jennifer felt the cold champagne in her mouth and was thinking that he didn't have a clue as to how far apart they soon would be.

"Now my darling, tell me everything. I heard Dimitri was very pleased with you."

Jennifer took the signed bank transfer paper out of her purse and showed it to Javier. "Isn't this what you wanted? $100 million to be transferred to Cordova investments? I did it for you, Javier. Are you happy?"

"Jennifer, my darling, you didn't do it for me, this was for you. He's moving the money to you for investment. I was only trying to help you."

"Javier, I went over to Europe for you. Don't you remember, you told me that with his investment in Cordova, we would make more money than we could ever dream of?"

"No my darling, this was all for you, I have only been trying to encourage you along. You were so determined to meet with Dimitri. Cordova Investments had nothing to do with it. We are merely a hedge fund for our select clientele. We certainly had nothing to gain with your affiliation with Dimitri."

Javier was not responding to her as she had expected. In fact, he was making statements that didn't reflect any of their prior activities.

Before she had another chance to continue to draw Javier out and reveal his scheme, he grabbed her, placing a firm kiss on her lips. Maybe it was her imagination, but he seemed to be handling her roughly.

"Bellissima, I've missed you so much. Let's not discuss business anymore. We need to focus on each other, not the pettiness of your business dealings. Come with me, I have a surprise for you."

All Jennifer needed was another surprise. She couldn't imagine what Javier had in store for her. Grabbing her hand, he led her outside. "Look, mi amor, I bought this for us." Docked next to the seawall behind the pool was a spectacular 125 foot yacht. "My darling, the best cure for jet lag is a little sea air. Let's try it out. You will love it."

If he was as dangerous as the FBI depicted him to be, the last thing Jennifer wanted to do was go on a cruise with Javier. Plus once they left land, she assumed that the wire would stop transmitting their conversations. Javier walked up the gangway, holding his hand out to Jennifer to join him. Out of desperation to buy some time, she said, "Javier, such a big, beautiful boat must need a captain."

"No bellissima, I can navigate the yacht myself. You will see, once we get going, I just turn on the auto-pilot. Jennifer, why do you look so glum? You should be happy that we are together again and going on a beautiful cruise. Maybe, my darling, we will even 'christen' the boat in the owner's stateroom."

"But Javier, I hate to take you away from your work. It's a weekday, why don't we plan a cruise over the weekend?"

"My darling, I want to be nowhere else but with you today."

They walked the few steps up to the bridge where Javier took the seat behind the controls. Putting on a captain's hat, he gave her a wink and started the diesel engines. As they were pulling away from the wharf, Jennifer felt sick to her stomach. She thought twice about running off the boat and swimming back to shore.

"Mi amor, please make yourself comfortable. There's a fridge right here stocked with champagne and wine."

"No Javier, I'll wait."

As the boat motored farther and farther from shore, Jennifer only became more apprehensive. She was praying that the FBI agents that were surveilling them would figure out what happened and track them down. When they approached an access to the ocean, Javier turned the bow of the boat out to sea.

"Javier, I thought we were just going to cruise down the Intracoastal? I get seasick easily, and would hate to throw up on your new boat. Can't we just stay in the calmer waters?"

Javier maintained the same course saying, "My darling, as I told you before, the sea air will do you good. If it's too choppy, we'll turn around. Not to worry."

It appeared to Jennifer as though they were heading right toward the Gulfstream. All Jennifer knew about it was that it was a favorite destination of fishermen. After cruising for a good 45 minutes, she saw Javier pull back the throttle and turn off the engines. Turning around to her he said, "You see my darling, look how beautiful it is out here."

As far as Jennifer could see, there wasn't a soul around. Not even a distant fishing boat. The agents would never find them here. She was becoming more anxious and fearful by the moment. Grabbing her hand strongly, Javier said, "Let me give you a tour of our new boat. You know I named it 'Mucho Dinero.' Do you like that name?"

Jennifer tried to conjure up a smile. He led her downstairs to a small living room area and then to the well equipped galley. Going down a few more steps, he showed her the various bedrooms. "And now my darling, I've saved the best for last." Opening two double doors, he said, "This is the Owner's Suite." To her surprise, as he opened the doors, she saw Mercedes sitting on the bed with a big smile on her face.

"Jennifer, I'm so happy to see that you've finally made it on board." What was Mercedes doing here? There must have been a reason why Javier had never told her. Jennifer could sense the tension mounting. Mercedes walked over to her with her arms extended appearing to give her a hug. Instead, she put her hands under Jennifer's dress and grabbed the wire out. "You little bitch; you have turned on us, the ones who have helped you the most. Unfortunately, you must pay for what you have done."

Jennifer started to panic, turning around she tried to run out of the suite, only to be blocked by Javier. "Bellissima, don't be afraid. Just stay calm and everything will be all right."

Before she knew what was happening, Mercedes was tying Jennifer's hands behind her back with duct tape. "Mercedes, why are you doing this to me?"

"Jennifer you have betrayed us and it is you who will pay for what you have done." Everything the FBI had told Jennifer about them was flashing back in her head. They were definitely on a mission to kill her.

Not saying a word, they each got on either side of her and led her back up to the top deck of the boat. Jennifer was squirming so much that they ended up dragging up to the stern of the boat. After throwing her onto a padded seat, Javier reached down under the seat and pulled out an anchor with heavy chains attached to it. Jennifer futilely started screaming for help. Starting to cry, she said to Javier, "I thought you loved me. How can you hurt me now? I have done nothing to hurt you."

She was pleading with him as he started to wrap the chains around her legs. "Javier, listen to me!"

"Shut up bitch!" Mercedes shouted at her.

"Javier, listen to me. I love you. Please don't hurt me!"

Ignoring her pleas, Javier said to Mercedes, "You grab her arms and I'll pick up her legs with the anchor and we'll just drop her overboard. The weight will carry her down."

Jennifer frantically was trying to move her body off the seat so she would fall on the floor of the boat, making it more difficult for them to lift her overboard. Just as Mercedes shouted at her again, "Bitch, stop moving!" there was the roar of two helicopters overhead. Simultaneously, four police patrol boats surrounded the yacht. Police were standing on the boats with their guns drawn. An officer with a megaphone shouted, "Raise your arms in the air now or we will shoot."

Javier and Mercedes immediately put their arms up, letting go of Jennifer. The police patrol boats quickly tied up next to the yacht. Several uniformed officers jumped onboard, while the others still had their guns drawn, and two officers soon handcuffed Javier and Mercedes. A third rushed over to Jennifer untying her hands and unwrapping the chains fastening the anchor around her legs. "Are you all right, Miss?" he asked.

"I'm fine. I can't believe you were able to find me."

"Even though we were unable to receive any transmission from the wire once you left shore, we were able to track your movements through a GPS chip that was embedded in the device."

Shivering with shock, Jennifer said, "Thank God. You saved my life. Thank you for being here. They were just about to throw me overboard."

Draping a blanket around her shoulders, the officer said, "You're safe now, Miss. It seems as though your nightmare has finally come to end."

Jennifer watched as the officers were taking the handcuffed Javier and Mercedes off the boat. Javier was shouting to her, "Bellissima, this was all a misunderstanding. We were just playing a little joke on you."

All Jennifer could reply to him was, "Thanks for the great ride." Moments later the boats sped off heading to the shore, carrying their treacherous prisoners.

Two of the officers stayed on the yacht comforting her, while a third navigated the vessel back to the Police Patrol headquarters.

When they finally made it back to shore, Inspector Handler and Agent Grimes were awaiting their arrival at the dock. After Jennifer walked off the yacht onto the gangway, she fell into Inspector Handler's arms and started crying. "I've never been so afraid in my life."

"Miss Palmer, you are a brave young woman and we thought you would like to know about Dimitri. He's had a long term relationship with the FBI. He has been a great asset to the United States. Behind the scenes, he played a very important role in saving your life. Agent Grimes will take you back home to your parents who I'm sure will be elated to see you alive and well."

As Jennifer got into Grimes' car, she thought to herself, about the whirlwind of events that she had experienced over the past year. Despite it all, she had tasted the sweet elixir of success. She was now more determined than ever to shine; no matter what it takes...

Epilogue

Jennifer Palmer testified against Javier Cordova and Mercedes Cambridge during their jury trial.

She was suspended from the securities industry by FINRA for a period of two months. Her Series 7 license was subsequently re-instated.

She was able to keep a portion of the commissions generated from her association with Cordova Investments due to the fact that those trades were deemed to be legitimate.

Jennifer moved backed to Coconut Grove, purchasing a town house near her parents' home.

She is currently employed at Tate Yardley as a broker in good standing and is speaking publicly to women's groups about the topic of personal empowerment.

Javier Cordova was found guilty of money laundering and financial fraud as well as one count of attempted murder. He is serving a 25 year sentence in a Federal penitentiary. Since his incarceration, his high priced attorney assures him that his case will be heard on appeal within a year's time.

Mercedes Cambridge was found guilty as an accomplice to money laundering, financial fraud and one count of attempted murder. She is serving out a 20 year sentence at a Federal penitentiary. She will be eligible for parole in 10 years.

Dimiti Stravinsko is still the largest producer of Russian vodka and has taken up permanent residence in the principality of Monaco. Periodically, he is engaged by the FBI or Interpol for his assistance in sting operations.